T0281803

The Cholla Kid

Center Point
Large Print

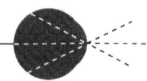

**This Large Print Book carries the
Seal of Approval of N.A.V.H.**

The Cholla Kid

JACKSON COLE

CENTER POINT LARGE PRINT
THORNDIKE, MAINE

This Center Point Large Print edition
is published in the year 2020 by arrangement with
Golden West Literary Agency.

Copyright © 1935 by A. Leslie Scott.
Copyright © 1935 under the title COWBOYS REVENGE
in the British Commonwealth.
Copyright © renewed 1968 by A. Leslie Scott.

Originally published in the US by G. Howard Watt.
Originally published in the UK by Cassell.

The text of this Large Print edition is unabridged.
In other aspects, this book may vary
from the original edition.
Printed in the United States of America
on permanent paper.
Set in 16-point Times New Roman type.

ISBN: 978-1-64358-577-2 (hardcover)
ISBN: 978-1-64358-581-9 (paperback)

The Library of Congress has cataloged this record under
Library of Congress Control Number: 2019957008

CONTENTS

CHAPTER I
THE RATTLE OF GUNFIRE

MOONLIGHT sifted down through the pine trees. The eerie cry of a hoot owl quivered lonesomely to a dim echo. The crackle of dry twigs and the muted clomp of a horse's hoofs in the thick red dust of the trail were the only sounds.

Night in the Ramireñas, and Ace Sutton, better known in the country west of New Mexico's Pecos as the Cholla Kid, frowned into the gloom, realizing that he was still a long, long way from where he had hoped to be when the night shadows fell.

Riding at a slow gait, Ace came out of the last red gullies of the mountainous hills behind him. He was headed for the flatlands which for a long time had lain ahead, blisteringly, under the coppery sun—apparently near but deceivingly far away. Beyond them lay the desert town of Hondo, the Cholla Kid's destination—Hondo, the town of far-flung ill repute. But whether it was the hole-in-the-ground dusty cowtown where rumor said swaggering gun-slingers drank and prowled and where death lay in wait, or whether it was only the usual gathering place for sun-scorched cowmen from the outlying ranges, the Cholla Kid now realized that, at nightfall, it was some distance ahead. How far, the man on the pinto pony did not know.

A matter of greater consequence for the moment occupied him. His pressing need was for water. It had been for more than the hour it had taken him to emerge from the last cooling shadows of the Ramireña Hills to trail down into the rutted dust of the road to Hondo, watching the flare of colors that shot across the horizon, blazoning the setting of the sun, and then cataclysmic nightfall. Darkness, except for the glimmer from a moon just above the horizon—moonlight that would not last long—and the pinto Jerky still without water. His heaving sides were panting for it, even at the slow pace. The last drop in Ace Sutton's canteen had gone somewhere back there in the red gullies that were dry and seared.

The moonlight flickering on the rider's worried face showed him to be a man who blended well with the country through which he was riding. A true son of the Southwest, the Cholla Kid was lean, muscled, and as rugged as the Ramireña Hills through which he had just passed. Not more than twenty-five years old, there was a touch of the dare-devil in his keen gray eyes. A love of life and for adventurous quest danced in their depths when they were not, when occasion demanded, like cut steel; merciless.

In dusty chaps, beneath which were dustier high-heeled boots with roweled Mexican spurs, his lean waist was encircled by a gun belt from which black-stocked Colts hung against either hip. A flopping sombrero was atop his black head—hair that the moonlight showed raven, and none of the clinging red dust. Cowboy, man of the desert and of the ranges, was etched in every lineament and in each habiliment. There was no mixture about Ace Sutton. He was all cow country. His pony, Jerky, dust-streaked now, but whose coat was usually sleek and glossy, was also all cow country.

Jerky's eyes were bright and alert, in spite of the day's long trek. His ears were pointed and sensitive. He flicked one of them back inquiringly when Ace, noting the loping cottontails and gray-ghost shapes of coyotes cringing away at sight of them—a sign that to the cowboy meant water somewhere near—muttered something.

"Nothin' gets by you, does it, old scout?" Ace said aloud.

He was long used to speaking his inmost thoughts to the pinto he rode. Jerky understood. He flicked the other ear as Ace told him:

"Goin' to turn off here a spell, feller—see if we can find some o' that water your tongue's hangin' out for. And if them cottontails are not lyin', why—"

Jerky's answer was a soft snort of approval

for a reasonable suggestion. Leaving the rutted road, Ace turned off into another gulley, the last probably before he should reach the flatlands. The long, cooling fingers of night were spreading over them now. Travelling would be easier.

Along the dry-wash bottom that cut into the last rolling foothills of the Ramireñas, Ace guided his pony slowly. His keen eyes watched for the signs of the water he was certain must soon appear.

The moon's brief appearance for that night was almost over, its dim light fading from the gulley, when suddenly the pinto thrust forward his ears. His nostrils quivered. Ace grinned through his drying lips.

"Got it, Boy?" he asked. "Guess maybe you have. We been passin' through the rabbit brush a while now—ought to be."

He lifted in his stirrups, peering ahead, listening, as he pulled in on his reins. The pinto halted obediently. From ahead, around a pile of boulders, came the welcome, unmistakable sound of trickling water. Ace nodded as he loosened his reins.

"Right you are!" he commended. "Go to it, Jerky. I'd sure admire to fill up with you."

Moonless night had covered hills and flatlands like a black veil of heavy gauze through which silver points of stars flickered when Ace Sutton, refreshed by long libations of the clear spring water, and from his rest in the long grass beside the spring, again topped his pinto. Time to amble along toward Hondo.

He had intended to reach the town he knew by its reputation only along about sundown. Now it would be well along in the night when he got there, even if the town were no further away than he figured. He was considering the advisability of bedding down for the night, and going on in the morning as Jerky mosied along, choosing his own trail. When the pinto chose to jog along the dry-wash and on up and out toward the flatlands and the Hondo road, Ace decided to go on. He settled down to his ride.

With thoughts of the town in his mind, what he had heard of it, and his own reason for heading in its direction, the cowboy did not at first notice when Jerky began to show signs of uneasiness. He recognized it when for the third time the pony turned back his ears toward his rider. Ace knew that meant a question. When there came no answering touch on reins, the pinto gave a sudden low snort. The questioning ears shot forward, pointing stiffly dead ahead.

Ace knew the meaning of that. Something, somebody, was ahead in the shadows. The keen senses of the pony had discovered it before his less observant rider had.

Ace jerked straight in his saddle, taut and listening, hand moving swiftly to gun-butt. His eyes searched swiftly along the gulley, up the canyonlike slope and to the ridge above. Against the lighter starred sky the rocks, gray in the daylight, were now black silhouettes. There was no movement anywhere, no sign of moving figure, man or animal.

He spoke to Jerky in a low voice:

"What is it, Boy? What you see?"

Again the almost imperceptible snort, air gently whistling through nostrils wide and quivering, ears straight to the front and unmoving. Jerky, at a dead standstill at the head of the gulley, kept up his alert watch. Slowly Ace got from his mount's back, cautiously moving him farther back into the shadows.

"If you're lyin' to me, Jerky, old-timer," he whispered sternly, "you're goin' to be a plumb sorry hoss."

He tightened his gun belt and slipped along the sheltered side of the gulley. There was no prevarication in Jerky, as Ace shortly discovered. Slipping back down the gulley toward the spring, he saw that its walls were not unbroken as he had at first thought, but that not far from where his pinto had stopped, another gulley cut into it, hidden by undergrowth. From what he could guess in the dark, it led to the rocky canyon higher up and behind the flatlands.

A trail it seemed to be, and as his eyes searched along the thin line that showed beside the black of the shrubbery, he saw a shelf that stood out, gray-black. Along the shelf a man was moving. Ace was near enough to hear an occasional crunch of gravel beneath the man's boots. He plainly made out the silhouette of a bulky figure in a black sombrero, the type of figure who could be law-bringer or law-breaker.

Making no slightest sound, Ace watched, but the next moment the man on the shelf had gone on. He disappeared around a fissure in the rock. The watcher in the gulley pushed his dusty hat back from a black wing of travel-damped hair, and breathed deep of the cool air that was settling in the bottom of the gulley. He shook his head as he moved cautiously back to his horse.

"Somebody sneakin' aroun' a-watchin', huh? Couldn't have been for me . . . But the question is, did he see me?"

There was slight doubt in the Cholla Kid's mind that the man, whoever he was, had seen. In fact, he might have been up there on that shelf all the time Ace and Jerky had been resting beside the spring. Why the bulky man had been there, the black-haired cowboy had no idea; nor did he care. It was annoying, nevertheless. He had hoped to reach Hondo without his coming being heralded.

Anyway the man was gone now, and it was unlikely he would see him again. It looked like he was on some kind of business that would not bear the light of day, at that, sneaking along in the rocks, with his horse hidden out somewhere.

There was only a silvery glow to show that the moon had shown its face at all when Ace rode out through a shallow notch and came again to the stretch of dried grass land that led him onto the Hondo road he had quitted in search of water. The flatlands lay murkily ahead. For a time no sound came to him but the familiar clop-clop of Jerky's ambling hoofs, and the small night sounds which to the cowboy, familiar with them, held no more significance than the light whimper of the slight night breeze.

Gradually—and he could not have told when or how he sensed it—it was borne in on him that he was not travelling through the night alone. Somewhere not far away, where, he did not as yet know, there were others—men riding. His keen instinct told him that soon his ears would confirm his suspicion.

His senses alert, he went slowly on. Sounds that grew and took form told him he was right. He was not the only rider along that lonely road that night. Suddenly, drifting his pony to a soundless walk along the dim, dusty ribbon unravelling toward Hondo, he reined up to listen as a new sound reached his ears. There was a rider on the trail ahead, travelling in the same direction as Ace. If it were, by chance, the man he had seen back on the rim of the small canyon, it was evident there was no longer any interest in the movements of the Cholla Kid. Else, the rider would not have been ambling along ahead like that.

Cholla nodded, and his eyes narrowed. Whoever he was, that rider was taking no particular pains to get anywhere in a hurry, nor to keep his presence from being known. The click of hoofs against stone came clearly to Cholla's ears, and through the night air there drifted to his nostrils the easily distinguishable smell of tobacco smoke.

The lean, dark-haired horseman bestriding Jerky was not particularly pleased with his discovery. He went on though, but more carefully than ever, taking canny care that the man ahead of him should not suspect his presence in the Hondo road. There were those who had called the Cholla Kid reckless, but Cholla did not play cards at night, in a strange country, with strangers.

The shadowy flatlands were nearer, marked with squares of black that were alfalfa, and with queer shapes. Behind and to the southwest ran the jagged silhouette of the Ramireña Hills. Northward, the fanged ramparts of the Cinchitos etched the skyline, dim against the starred expanse. A wild, a rugged, a silent land, far from ranch house or town, a spot where anything might happen.

With Jerky's hoofs barely moving ahead as the pinto lifted them daintily and set them down almost soundlessly, as though he divined his rider's unspoken words for caution, Cholla deftly twisted a brown paper cigarette and expertly lit the quirly beneath the cover of his horsehide coat, all his senses lynx-sharp. The night was just a little too ominously quiet and mysterious to suit him, the horseman ahead too much like an unseen wraith. Moreover, the shadowy man he had seen on the rock shelf was not sufficiently explainable. His acute sixth sense, which had ever stood by him and which he always heeded without questioning, was buzzing a warning rattle.

Swiftly, unexpectedly, his hunch materialized. Jerky's head came up sharply. He came to a halt without warning. Cholla stiffened in his saddle, straining forward, listening. His hand went out to touch the pinto's neck.

"Steady, Boy," he soothed, his voice a sibilant whisper. "Hist!"

Legs stiffened on hearing the warning under-tone, Jerky stood as still as the trees beside the road. Cholla's head bent forward, his ears cocked, listening. He had caught a dim rumble borne down the wind—sounds coming from the trail ahead. Ugly sounds, sudden and abrupt, like the churn and boil of horses' hoofs; hoarse words, with an attempt to keep voices down.

Then swift mêlée! One suddenly raised voice—a shout of anger! Above it arose the terrified scream of a horse in mortal agony. Silence then, as swiftly as had come the sound of turmoil in the darkness. Not a whisper through the breeze. There was trouble ahead on the road up there—bad trouble!

Quickly and silently Cholla backed his pinto into the shrubbery alongside the strip of road, deep with rusty-hued dust. For five leaden minutes he waited there, hidden in the inky shadows of a greasewood clump. The sounds of moving horses again then, through the awed silence. Horsemen were cautiously moving southward through the flatlands. It was impossible to gauge their number, but they were a group. Unmoving, Cholla heard the sounds die to uncertain faintness, then fade away altogether, until from across the flats there was once more only the whisper of the night breeze.

For a short moment only that silence lasted, long enough for Cholla to move out into the road, still hesitating whether to go ahead. Then the silence was jarringly shattered by a fusillade of shots. On the heels of the volley came the muffled, far-off tattoo of fast-travelling ponies, and a single gunshot's echo that undulated across ridge and flat and was taken up at last by the peaks of the Ramireñas. Then the distant boil of sound was merged for the last time into silence, grim now, and menacing.

CHAPTER II
A GRUESOME FIND

IT WAS a silence so deep that the Cholla Kid, hidden in the greasewood clumps, could hear the regular thumping of the pinto's heart against his sides. His own breathing sounded stentorious in that silence that was not one that brought fear to his heart, but rather the awesome silence of lonely places.

"I don't know what this is all about," Cholla grunted to Jerky's pricked ears, "but I'm bettin' it ain't accordin' to Hoyle, whatever the cards say. Shore sounds like dirty work at the crossroads."

Hesitating no longer, he touched his pony's flanks and in a moment they were breezing along the trail at a fast clip. He soon came across plenty of evidence that his hunch had been right. Trampled earth at a spot around the first bend, a broken greasewood limb, hoof-bruised 'squite grass. Men had been there, more than two or three of them, their horses milling while they had been in confab, or about some nefarious business veiled by the darkness.

The match the cowboy struck to investigate the ground burned his fingers before he tossed it away and straightened up in his saddle. His thinned lips had grown thinner, a tight line. His eyes were narrower and there was no care-free glimmer in them; only steely depths.

"Uh-huh," he breathed softly, nodding at his own conclusions. "Reckon now I'll just have a little look-see over yonder way where I heard those hombres headin'. I've heard a good and plenty about the town of Hondo and this here Comal Valley—looks like some folks wasn't maybe lyin' when they tagged it the Hub o' Hell." He grinned wryly as he turned toward his mount. "I got a plumb good hunch I'm goin' to enjoy this visit o' mine to this particular wrinkle of Texas. Yeah."

He swung a leg across Jerky's back, touching the reins for him to go ahead.

"Yeah," he repeated to the pinto through his tight lips, "it might be I'd have a little chore or so to 'tend to around here, Boy, should it turn out you and me don't have no call to fan the trail for a doctor. Some things hereabouts might be needin' a little ironin' out. Same as you work the kinks out o' the tough muscles of a wall-eyed mustang on coolish mornin's."

They had moved on but a few paces when the pony again stopped suddenly short without warning, ears pointed forward, breath snorting through flared nostrils. Cholla swung to the ground then, dropped his reins over his mount's head, and crept ahead silently, keeping in the shadows of the grease-wood clumps and mesquite, hugging the brush.

Through the darkness came a low whinny, followed by a confused scrambling somewhere not far ahead. Jerky, Cholla realized quickly, had been aware of the presence of another horse, even before his master had heard a sound.

The cowboy stopped short, his capable fingers gently tapping the black gun-butt at his waist. Then he smiled grimly and moved forward. Taking all that caution for nothing! Why hadn't his second thought been his first? A horse tangled up in a picket rope, of course. That must be it, but still Cholla's senses were alive to the last cell as he went on, just in case . . . And one of the black-butted .45s was not in its holster at his belt. It was in his hand.

Moving as cautiously as he could through the faintly cut darkness, he came abruptly to the sharp rim of a barranca which dropped sheerly down to a considerable depth. Sinking to the ground, he hooked his head over the edge and stared downward. In the black shadows at the cut's bottom he could see nothing. He had to risk a light, and struck a match, shielding it between his cupped palms. A low grunt escaped his lips as his gaze pinched and focused. Even that meager light, a flickering match flame, had shown him in twenty seconds all that he needed to see.

At the bottom of the deep wash loomed the vague bulk of a big roan horse that was trying to struggle to his feet, whinnying pathetically as he was unable to do so. There was a human-like pleading in the animal's whinny when he caught Cholla's scent.

And fifteen feet beyond the struggling animal sprawled the still figure of a man!

As high up as he was, and in the darkness, it was impossible for the cowboy to tell whether the man was alive, but the Cholla Kid had encountered enough such like "accidents" in his life to realize that help must not be long delayed. On the instant he was dropping over the rim. With all speed possible, he made his way down into the barranca. His feet finally reaching its flat, rocky bottom, gingerly he picked his way through the scattered boulders and cactus clumps matting it, and approached the floundering horse from the rear.

He quickly swept the horse with a glance as he stumbled hastily on. That quick survey showed him that the animal's right foreleg and left hindleg were broken. What was more revealing and plainly to be seen at close quarters in the barranca bottom was that there was a deep bullet crease across the animal's rump.

Cholla's lips tightened grimly as he swung on away toward the limp form of the man sprawled beyond. It was grotesquely twisted in the rocks.

And that bullet gouge on the horse knocked into a cocked hat any notion the Cholla Kid might have had that the splendid roan gelding had blundered over the edge of the wash in the dark.

Bending over the sprawled man, Cholla turned him over on his back. He thumbed a light and looked down at the waxen, blood-stained face. Nothing more anybody could do for that poor hombre in this world, except to see that he got decent burial—if he deserved it. But there was something about the man that told Cholla he had been a victim, unquestionably, of some of the fine and fancy murdering coyotes who made the Hub of Hell their headquarters.

The cowboy knew the man was beyond aid even before he made his quick explorations for certainty. No pulse; no heartbeat. The man, past middle age and graying at the temples, who had been tumbled among the rocks, was stone dead. Not yet cold, and Cholla himself had heard the mêlée in which he had met his death. A deep and jagged cut was across the murdered man's head and it was crushed. One of his arms was shattered.

Recognizing that there was nothing he could do, unless it were still possible for him to pick up some clue that would lead to the murderers, Cholla got to his feet. With low, muttered oaths he set to work. First, of course, for the suffering gelding. He had taken a half dozen steps toward the roan and his gun was half lifted when as suddenly he lowered it, reminded of Jerky. It would not do to have his pony stampeding up there on the edge of the barranca, alone, and startled as he would be by another shot. He must get Jerky down there someway. Besides there might be a chance he would need him in a hurry.

Cholla glanced swiftly about him, searching for a way out of the barranca other than the way he had come into it. It took keen searching in the darkness, but shortly he located the spot where the up-trail left the coulee on the south slope, and also where it might be entered further back in the direction of where he had left his mount. That would be satisfactory. They could leave the coulee by the up-trail, but the Cholla Kid did not mean to quit that spot until he had made a thorough search of the barranca and vicinity.

It was easier getting back to the pinto by way of the trail than it had been climbing down, hanging to trailing bushes and jutting boulders. Within minutes he was leading Jerky into the barranca, and up to the gelding which had fallen back, quivering with pain. Holding his paint's reins in his left hand, to reassure him by his own nearness at what he was going to hear, Cholla approached the injured roan, again drawing his pistol. The least he could do, now that the man who had ridden the gelding was gone, was to put the poor brute out of its misery, discover what he could about what had happened, then trail on into Hondo and report his findings to the sheriff. Murder had been committed in the Comal Basin that night, and dirty murder at that.

Halting a couple of feet from the stricken horse, he sent a swift, accurate slug between its eyes. Without a sound the roan fell over on its side, the satiny limbs jerked once or twice, then he was still. Startled at the suddenness of the roar that split the silence, Cholla's pinto snorted at the thunder of the .45 and tried to rear. The cowboy held fast, and with a short tug of the reins, quieted him. Leaving him ground-hitched then, quivering but quiescent, the Cholla Kid took up the search of the barranca to see if by chance the murderers had left a clue.

Meticulously he went over the bottom of the wash for twenty feet in every direction of the dead man, searching for sign of a weapon, for anything else, but found nothing. There was no sign of a gun, nor were there even fresh hoof prints. Cholla was certain that he had left no stone in the barranca bottom in the prescribed space unsearched when finally, meeting with no success, he returned to his rein-hobbled pinto. And he had just two matches left. Those he must conserve—for some other emergency. It seemed to be a night for them.

It had been a night for murder, that was certain, and though the Cholla Kid had not actually seen it committed, he could almost claim to have been a witness. Which he would not, unless something unforeseen made such a course necessary. In making his report to Hondo's sheriff he had better let it be supposed he had stumbled on the dead man while making his way through the barranca for a short cut to the south trail.

Cow-country-bred as he was, and no stranger to range violence, what had happened was plain to Cholla. He could reconstruct the scene that had occurred in the dark, mentally vision the tragic drama. He had no idea who the dead man was, but it was certain to him that the grizzled victim was a cowman who had been gulched from behind. That, so he had been informed, was one of the Comal Valley's favorite little jests.

Jerky was still trembling and dancing about nervously when Cholla approached, surprisingly to the cowboy who had never known the pinto long to exhibit signs of temperament. Cholla reached for the reins.

"Hold it, Jerky," he growled to the snorting pony, lifting a booted foot to a stirrup. "What the hell—"

For the pinto did not quiet at the sound of the Cholla Kid's voice, except momentarily. Then he snorted again, squatted, and wheeled, swinging Cholla completely around with his turn. And even as Cholla's sixth sense flashed a sudden warning and his hand streaked for his holstered gun, black danger sprang to being on the barranca rim above. In the wan light of the prairie stars studding the cloud-veiled sky, his keened eyes made out the sooty silhouettes of three men crouched up there, guns in hand and trained down on him. And as he raked a look upward, a hoarse, grating voice called out:

"Stay hitched jest where you are, you damned murderin' skunk! Git them hands up before you keel over with lead poisonin'! Git 'em up, I said! Plenty high!"

A quick thinker by nature, Cholla had never been a whit less slow in action. He was not now. Brain and muscle moved in swift accord, perfectly co-ordinated. With him to decide, was to act on the instant. A pantherish leap landed him in his saddle. He bent far over the horn and jammed home his long-roweled Mex spurs. The paint pony lifted on all fours to come down in his stride, streaking up the barranca like a red-and-white flash splitting through the shadows.

All hell broke loose above. A high-pitched yell cut the night. A raucous voice bellowed, "Stop right where you are, you!" Another screeched shrilly, "Damn, he's gettin' away! Get him!"

The surprised yells came before any shots. Cholla's sudden action had for the moment dumbfounded the three on the barranca's rim. But only for a split second. A gun crashed then, pluming a roaring wink of scarlet at the Cholla

Kid; another. The fusillade became a blast and a belch of pistol roar thundering after the flying paint pony. Jerky was running with belly close to the ground. The darkness was lanced by splitting flames.

Bent low and against the off side of his saddle, Indian fashion, the Cholla Kid rode like a devil possessed. Singing lead thudded metallically against the barranca walls and zipped like mad hornets about him as he raced up the stony bottom, a cold gun clutched in his fist. No time to shoot. He would only be wasting bullets which might soon be sorely needed if he sent any back at that rim where three men were determined to have his life. But he was thanking his lucky stars that he knew where to find the trail for which he was heading.

"Climb, Jerky, climb!" he cried, raking in his spurs as they plunged through the undergrowth screening it.

Eyes narrowed to slits and his mouth a thin gash, Cholla flung a look across his shoulder as the stout pinto lunged upward, shoes flailing the rocks into glinting sparks. Jerky was straining to his utmost, uncannily as aware as the man who rode him that death swung in swift behind.

Above the muscle-stretch and heave of his pony, Cholla heard the drumming of pursuing hoofs racing along the opposite side of the draw. His lips drew into a grin of grimness, recognizing that his moment of grace had been the infinitesimal time the shooting men had taken to leap to and straddle their mounts. Once up the barranca side, he was certain he would have a chance, since his swift investigation of the place had shown him no break on the rim where the pursuers had been that would lead them down into and across the draw. They might have to ride for miles before they could get across to Cholla's side.

For a good pair of miles he pushed the paint for all the horse was worth. When he did draw off and stop to let Jerky blow, through the still air he could barely hear the faint thud of hoofs to the northeast. The pursuit had not been given up, but it sounded to the intently listening cowboy as though his pursuers had got on the wrong track in the darkness, after they had reached the end of the barranca. Most probably they were now combing the flats between there and Hondo for him. He chuckled grimly, thankful that he had let Jerky have his head in taking a wide, roundabout course.

Squatting on his haunches after he had dismounted and loosened the saddle girths to give the pinto his well-deserved chance for getting back his wind, he made and smoked a welcome quirly. He grinned crookedly and thinly as the small sounds of pursuit came to his ears from the distance. A fat chance those slunkheads had now of rounding him up in the open and tagging him with their iron. He would match his gun against any of theirs, though as yet he had had no chance, in this encounter, to let its fire search out human flesh. And he would match his paint-bronc against any cayuse ever forked. Jerky had once again proved his fleet-footed worth.

Cholla's thoughts were grim, though, as he figured out the probable reason for the attack upon him. In all likelihood the trio who had sneaked up on him so noiselessly knew plenty about the dead man in the barranca. For all he knew, one of them might have been the man he had seen back on the ledge at the water hole. That hombre had not been hunting in the dark for stray cattle. From where he sat, it looked much to Cholla as though he had appeared at the opportune time—for the killers—to have a murder pinned on him.

Grinding out his cold brownie beneath a boot heel, the Cholla Kid got up lazily, forked his saddle and headed northeast in a long, wolfish lope. Luck staying with him he would be miles away from this section and the rattlesnakes who were so set on making him pinch hit for them in a murder he had not committed, before an hour had passed.

As he rode, his twitching nostrils winnowed the night air for trace of danger, and a smile twisted his lips. Sixth sense and self-protective instinct were working overtime.

CHAPTER III
CHOLLA FRAMES HIS ALIBI

THE inconstant moon that had favored the Cholla Kid when it had early sunk below the horizon had left no trace of its brief sojourn in the dark blue bowl of the sky. But the stars flickered more brightly, illumining the landscape dimly as Sanna Merrill, of the Rafter M ranch, stood in the doorway of the ranch house and gazed out into the darkness.

She was still dressed in the riding breeches, white shirt open at the neck, and bright-hued handkerchief draped about her firm, tanned young throat that had been her costume through hours of weary waiting and riding out in search of one who had not come.

Through the black of the night she was trying to pierce the shadows down a long coulee that stretched away from the house. Her eyes went from it to search across the flatlands, and the green range that lay black under the stars. Her ears were strained for sounds; but there was only silence.

Hours she had waited, knowing that her father, away on a mission that to them was all-important, should have reached the home ranch before sundown. It was nearing nine o'clock now and there was no sound of horse hoofs to tell her that he was approaching. Ever so often, since late afternoon, she had saddled her pony and ridden out, hoping to meet him. Now instinct was warning her that something had gone wrong.

Sanna tried to tell herself that her fears were foolish, groundless. She was only impatient. Dad was always telling her to have more patience, that everything would come out all right. But together they had waited so long for that happy time. It looked as if it would never come. They had worked, hoped, with their waiting for the right to prevail, but to Sanna it was beginning to look as if it were only those who were wrong, who took all they could get by any means at all, who ever got anywhere.

And this home of hers, this ranch . . . Oh, surely they would not have to give it up *now!* After all their struggles to make it what it was. Dad must be on his way back right now with the good news of his success. He had only met with some unforeseen delay, of course. He would laugh at her for being so worried, not even eating her supper.

Patience? Sanna smiled. It would take all the patience that could be mustered to keep on fighting against the devils who were so deter-mined to take from her father and her their lovely

Twin Springs country. It was a heart-breaking job, fighting against all the powers of evil that made the Comal Valley, with Hondo as its focal point, a place which right and honor seemed to have entirely passed by.

The ranch house was brightly lighted. Golden squares from the windows lay on the grass about it, but beyond all was dark. Sanna tried to make herself believe she saw some movement far off in the shadows, but sighed, knowing that she did not.

Supper had been ready for some time. Maria, the Mexican cook, Sanna's nurse in the childhood days not so long gone by, had tried to get the girl to eat, but without success. Sanna felt as if she could never eat until she heard her father's cheerful "Hello!" and knew that he was safely back. Standing in the doorway, she could hear, through the open hall door that led to the kitchen, the sizzling of potatoes in the frying pan as Maria prepared fresh ones. The smell of newly-made coffee would at any other time have been appetizing.

"Better come on and eat your supper, Sanna," old Maria called, poking her wrinkled face through the door opening. "Your *padre* would not like you should not eat. He will be here soon, *chiquita*."

When the girl did not come at the call, the old woman lumbered through the hallway to her, carrying a cup of coffee. At her insistence, Sanna drank it, but shook her head, refusing to be coaxed to eat. She gave back the empty cup and went on out into the warm dark. Fear was gnawing at her heart, and it made her want to be alone with the darkness.

The sagebrush-covered flats, softly lighted by the Texas stars, met and eddied into the dark green of alfalfa fields along the creek. They were a dusty pattern of gray and black. The night was still, and there seemed no sound at all except the distant yapping of coyotes, until from inside the house came the sudden dong of the clock striking nine, clear and ringing in the stillness. Shivering a little, Sanna leaned against a hewn post on the Rafter M ranch house and gazed off toward the far away Ramireñas, black phantoms in the night silence.

So deeply buried was she in her own thoughts that her ears, intently listening for familiar sounds, must have been closed to them for a few moments. She suddenly started and stared sharply, her reverie broken. The clop of a horse's hoofs against rock! Near at hand! A vague, dark shape was moving in the starlight. Sanna started forward, then shrank back against the post. The shape was in no way familiar. There was a clutch at her heart and she drew a quick, sharp breath of disappointment when she realized it was not her father.

Whoever it was, the horseman was approaching the adobe ranch house quietly and warily, his mount at such a slow, noiseless walk that it was not strange Sanna had not heard him when he had come across the grass. He was approaching over it at the extreme edge of the road and not along its dim yellow ribbon.

A frown of perplexity wrinkled the girl's brows as her eyes searched the oncoming rider. His behavior was queer. A stranger—obviously. What could he want? She straightened up, suspicious.

And no one knew better than the Cholla Kid who came on so slowly, riding Jerky cautiously toward the ranch house, that there was need for suspicions of night visitors in that country, strangers or not.

Cholla Sutton was not unaware of the shadow near the porch pillar as he reined in his pinto several yards from the steps. He knew, too, that strangers thereabouts needed to keep a wary eye, and that he was taking a chance in visiting a ranch house about which he knew nothing, whose occupants might turn out to be anything but friendly.

But the yellow glow of lamplight from its cheerful windows had beckoned him like a magnet as he jogged along a sandy trail off the Hondo wagon road. He was out of matches, too. That was his main reason for bracing the place, and whoever lived there should not object to a small kindly gesture like the gift of a few matches.

As he reined up, he raised his right hand, palm out, in the sign of peace known from Saskatchewan to Sonora.

"Hello, the house!" he called. "Can I make a little talk with the boss?"

"What is it?" replied the girl, not moving. "And name yourself."

Her voice . . . It startled Cholla for a moment. As much as it surprised him to discover that the dark shadow in what appeared to be man's clothing was a girl. But he answered at once, grinning friendly.

"I'm a stranger hereabouts," he explained. "Bound toward Hondo, but I must o' miscalculated some how long 'twould take me to get there. I'd shore appreciate a stake of matches, ma'am—I'm plumb out." He flashed his amiable smile at her. "Can do?"

The shadow stirred. It materialized from beside the porch pillar into the lithe form of a young girl, slim and youthful in her trim riding breeches. Her voice took on a more friendly cadence.

"Of course," she told him, almost hospitably. "Want to rest your saddle *poco tiempo* while I get them?" She hesitated a moment, glancing at him, sizing him up coolly. Before she turned she remarked casually: "Sit on the porch if you'd like—I'll be back in a minute."

Swinging down with a "Thank you kindly, ma'am," Cholla watched her enter the lighted doorway and disappear inside. His quick eye surveyed her, taking her in and cataloguing each feature and movement in a swift glance. If she had deigned to look back at him she would have seen pleased surprise in his gray eyes.

One glimpse had shown him her eyes were blue as sapphires. Her hair, softly golden brown, tumbled by the night breeze, whipped in curling tendrils about her healthily tanned oval face. Her throat was smooth beneath the opened shirt collar, her figure was slim and graceful and she was as light as thistledown as she sped away. Cholla, looking at her, had a queer feeling somewhere inside him, but his mind did not catalogue it. It was something new to him, different; another puzzle to iron out. If ever he got the chance.

He had dropped down on the porch step, but when she returned almost immediately with a handful of matches, he got up quickly. As she handed them to him, she asked casually:

"You say you're riding toward town? Did you follow the valley road from Encinal?"

"No, ma'am," lied Cholla promptly. For an hour he had been rehearsing the answer to just that question. His story was fixed in his mind. "I rode down from the Cinchitos—" gesturing toward the northern hills. "Reckon I got somewhat lost back there in the *brasada*, till I hit a trail a while ago. Sort of comes, I suppose, of tryin' to keep directions in your head, instead of jottin' 'em down on paper like I'd ought to have done, knowin' I was hittin' into a plumb strange neck o' the woods. But I come out all right—if I didn't go too far astray. Saw this light o' yours a ways back and jogged over. I shore thank you for these *fosforos*," he finished, pocketing the matches. "Got to needin' a quirly mighty bad about the time I discovered I didn't have no light . . . He glanced backward along the dark road, then at the girl. "How far is it to this here metropolis of Hondo?" he asked.

"Five miles," she answered shortly. "If you'd known this is the Rafter M, I suppose you'd have known that?" There was more than question in her voice. Almost accusation. Cholla got a quick impression that his story might not have gone over so good, or if it had, she still had her reasons for mistrusting him. Especially when she asked abruptly: "Ever been to Hondo, cowboy?"

Cholla did not miss the edge in her query. There had been a barb in her low, rich contralto voice; a trace of bitterness. He did not lift his eyes from the brown cigarette he had been making. Only shook his head.

"No'me," he said, touching match flame to his quirly top. "Never saw the town, nor none of this country. My first pasear down in this

38

neck o' Texas. I rode down from up Panhandle way. Sort o' got sand in my shoes, as you might say. Can't nowise seem to stay put . . . Always liked to have a look over the next hill. . . ." He laughed a little apologetically. "Reckon I'm *pre*-destined to jolt through life a-straddle the back of a cayuse."

Sanna stood motionless, watching him, searching him through and through. But her eyes, cool and appraising, did not show that she was noticing his splendid physique, nor his shining black hair, nor the gray eyes with the laughter in their depths. It was something beneath the surface for which she was looking.

"What are you figuring on doing in Hondo?" she asked suddenly. Her eyes never wavered from his as she added, slowly, a little scornfully: "Ride for a brand and hire out those six-shooters you wear thonged to your legs?"

Cholla chuckled, but refused to become indignant.

"You flatter me, ma'am," he told her, with a sweeping bow. "No, it's just like I said—I'm only driftin' along and lookin' over the country. Some time I might meet up with a layout I liked, and then I might sign on for a while before I'm taken with another attack of this wanderlust—it always happens that-a-way—but right now I'm free as air."

Sanna Merrill did not miss the quick, sardonic

smile that flashed over his dark features. She did not smile.

"Likely," she retorted coolly. "It's a good story you've got, if it is getting worn in spots. That's what all you imported trigger-twisters say." She turned her back for a swift moment, hesitated, then said rapidly: "But if you've got any gumption at all, ranny, I'd advise you to shy clear of Hondo and *keep on riding!*" Her lip curled. "None of my affair, of course, but that's for what it may be worth to you."

"A hellin' he-man's town, is it?" Cholla asked, with mock concern. "Well, well! You're gettin' me plumb int'rested, ma'am. Things have been gettin' right dull, just ridin' and eatin' and joggin' along—"

"Don't call me 'ma'am'!" she flared suddenly. "I don't like it."

"Then what'll it be?" he asked in feigned humility. "I'd shore be right proud to know— seein' I've got no kind of idea at all who hangs out at this Rafter M ranch of yours."

"My father owns the Rafter M," she announced with dignity. "He's Lynn Merrill. If you haven't heard of him, you probably will. I'm Sanna Merrill—" coolly, with smouldering anger in her eyes.

She took a step toward the open door, glancing at him sidewise, then at his pinto, ground-hitched nearby. Cholla appeared not to notice.

"Yeah," he said, his smile more friendly still. "Right glad to meet up with you, Miss Sanna Merrill. My name's Ace Sutton, in case you care to know it." He was moving a pace or two away from the steps as he nodded. "*Gracias* again for the matches."

"Don't mention it." She was studying him again, lip curling a little, eyes cold—eyes which, the cowboy had a quick thought, should never be icy like that, but always filled with light and laughter.

He shook his head slightly, grinned and moved back another step toward his mount. Jerky raised his rein-tied head inquiringly.

"By the way," the girl asked with frosty casualness, as she halted in the square of doorway that silhouetted her slenderness against the yellow lamplight, and she turned her head back over her shoulder toward Cholla, "did you happen to see anyone along the valley road tonight? Any rider travelling in this direction?"

"No'me." Cholla shook his head again with positiveness. "Wish I had—it's been plumb lonesome with nobody to say howdy to. I haven't seen nothin' but Mexicans and goats for the last couple o' days."

He ground out his quirly in the gravel under his heel and gathered up the paint's reins. Despite the cold casualness of the girl's words, there had been a nervous undercurrent of anxiety in them that Cholla was quick to catch. He hesitated, wondering just what to say, then lightly swung into the kak.

"Expectin' somebody that ain't turned up?" he asked, politely interested, jerking down the brim of his hat and settling himself into the leather.

"Perhaps," Sanna replied shortly. She added quickly, almost in the tone of a reprimand for his uncalled-for curiosity: "Glad to have met you, Mr. Sutton . . . Good-night."

"That goes double, Miss Sanna Merrill," replied Cholla, soberly. He ignored the stiffness of her statement and her manner. Then he laughed. "You know, I kinda like you in that get-up."

She saw his grin at the same moment he saw her angry frown. Without waiting for her retort, he kneed his paint pony and set off at a leisurely fox trot toward the road for Hondo.

The grin was wiped off his face, though, the moment his back was turned to the slender girl in the lighted doorway. Something else to be happening in one night. That girl was in trouble. That was plain. If Cholla's hunch was right, she had still deeper trouble coming to her. And something was telling him he was going to take a hand in the game in which she was playing with most of the cards stacked against her, and he was going to play it to the end.

He murmured to Jerky, as they jogged into the dim Hondo road:

"And what I'm sayin', Boy, is a girl like that oughtn't to get shoved into any such games, nohow."

CHAPTER IV
THE HUB OF HELL

IT WAS shortly after ten o'clock when the Cholla Kid topped the last rise in the road that led to Hondo. The town was spread out beyond in a bowl-like depression between the hills. In the distance, the scattered, squat buildings looked toylike. Cholla would have recognized the place for what it was without previous description—a desert cow-town that God had forgotten.

Like scores of other such towns that seemed fashioned from a worn and jagged-edged metal stamp and set carelessly down in the most available spot, Hondo, like a squatty, forbidding tarantula, sprawled Mex fashion about a dusty central plaza. Dark streets wriggled away from the square like a thousand-legged's feelers, shirttailing out where the mesquite and greasewood and chaparral crowded its purlieus.

Wagon roads and yellow-streaked trails radiated outward like the unevenly spaced spokes of a wheel. Some crawled across the saucer-like valley and up to the fringing hill ranges; others to diametrically opposed alfalfa land or to ravines aflame with *palo verde* blossoms. Some crept to low hills where gaunt desert growths clustered like sentinels warning of barrenness—catsclaw, *guajillo*, cacti and *ocotillo* with its surprisingly gardenia-textured flowers. And from some far-visioned chaos of ruptured rock, savage, thorny bushes and big *sahuarros* thrust up their spiked clubs jealously to guard a land nobody wanted to guard.

Set in the center of the greener land, Hondo, especially by night, was an evil-eyed, venomous thing unwinkingly charming with its beady eyes to cowmen and punchers from a big surrounding range land. To them it was the sinful mecca for all recreation.

Cholla jogged over the rise and ambled down the trail. He headed for the plaza. Lights were in most of the buildings. Only the one-story bank and a few false-fronted mercantile establishments were dark. Especially bright were the yellow shafts of light which marked the saloons. They spread out, fan-like, across the plaza and the board sidewalks.

Most of the town's activity was confined to its central portion. Crowds of people milled on the board walks and around the plaza. Spurred and sombreroed men with the mark of the range on them, flannel-shirted men, coatless and with low-swinging guns in gunbelts—men who made proud boast of being urban dwellers—and an occasional more snappily dressed gambler

46

and a scattering of women moved along and bantered. Some of the women, too fancifully dressed, walked smilingly along as if the town were theirs. Others, calico-clad, meekly making their way home with bundles and filled market baskets, stepped off the board walks to make way for their peacock sisters. There were few meek women who called Hondo home.

Reaching the edge of town, the Cholla Kid reconsidered his original intention of riding unconcernedly up to the plaza. Instead, he rode a circle around and north of the town where he pulled rein. Wrinkling his brows as he studied the town, he decided on another course. Moving on a few paces he slid into a dirty byway as black as crow's feathers and circled some more until he gained the Hondo-Seven Mile Pass road. That entered the town from the east. Gaining it, he rode along it carelessly, keeping up a jogging pace until he was once more in the town. Again he headed for the plaza.

Riding with deceptive indolence along the street, hat pulled low on his forehead, he scanned his surroundings at closer range with hard alertness. Hondo was going about its playtime business as he had at first seen it from a distance. Again he heard the jangle of music, fiddles from the saloons, and tinkling pianos; the click of roulette wheels; husky men's laughter.

Mongrel dogs barked at Jerky's heels as Cholla

came on, but the pinto ignored them as calmly as his rider ignored the occasional glances of curiosity accorded him as a stranger. The cowboy shoved on into the plaza and headed with unfailing accuracy toward the Legal Tender Saloon. Experience had given the Cholla Kid the instinct to make a bee line, in any town, for the town's main gathering place.

Tying his pinto at the rack, among tethered broncs from half a dozen outfits, Cholla clumped across the board sidewalk and let the green swinging doors of the Legal Tender slap shut behind him. He took in the scene with quick, shrewd comprehension as he strode across the boot-heel-and-spur-scarred floor to the bar. In one swift glance as he took his place with the bar loungers, he had sized them up. He could have accurately described each man present.

"Straight, with a chaser," he told the sleek bartender, promptly. Part Mex, that hombre, Cholla guessed—just a little too sleek. There were probably other interests in his mind besides shoving bottles and glasses across the mahogany.

From the moment he lined up at the bar he was aware that two men, standing near its far end, were watching him in the long mirror. One was a burly, thick-set hombre with a hard and seamed face, dark, stubbly jaw, and close-set eyes. Hardly the cowman type. His community status was hard to place.

There was something vaguely familiar to the cowboy in the man's set-up, but he could not place it—at first. But a swift stab of instinct, the urging of his sixth sense, told him that he had seen that man before. He had not seen his face, or he would have recalled it. It was the man's build, his bulk, that was familiar—as if Cholla had once glimpsed him at a distance; or in veiling shadows. He tried hard to place the fellow; could not. Well . . . nothing like being forewarned. If the man had also once seen the Cholla Kid, should now recognize him . . .

The other of the two watching men was a lean, lank, leatherfaced individual. Cholla had no instinct of ever having seen him before, but he was more easily placed. Some fifty years old, he had a scraggly, tobacco-stained mustache, and bleak blue eyes. A bone-handled .44 hung at his right hip. There was no need for the flip of the man's loose coat that showed the shiny star pinned conspicuously on his vest to know that he was the sheriff.

Cholla, apparently unconscious of their existence, could almost guess what the two men were saying.

"Know him?" the thickset man was asking.

As the Cholla Kid poured his second drink he noted that the man had a bullet scar along his jaw, and that the third finger of his right hand was missing.

49

The lanky, walrus-mustached sheriff shook his head.

"Nope. Never laid eyes on him before. Looks sorta salty, huh?"

"Looks ain't always what they seem," growled Scarface. The sheriff did not see his companion's heavy brows draw together as though he were, as was in fact the case, trying to remember just where he had seen that young cowpuncher before. It did not come to him at once. He glanced slyly into the mirror and laughed contemptuously. "Prob'ly one of them mail-house waddies. Think I'll brace him and find out somethin' or t'other. He may be totin' a star, savvy?"

The sheriff nodded. He "toted a star" himself, but no one knew better than he how unhealthy it would be for him or for those he served, the men who had put him and kept him in office, for any real upholder of the law to mingle in the affairs of Hondo. He gnawed a corner of his mustache as he advised:

"Yeah, shore he might be. You never can tell about some hombres. Reckon he can answer a few questions. Go right ahead, Zach—make him talk."

Zach Dagget hitched at his gun-belt, and swaggered away from the bar. He stopped idly at a green-baize-covered table to look over the shoulders of some cowboys with clinking spurs who were losing their monthly wages to the plaid-suited, fish-eyed gentleman who was running the game.

Sheriff Newt Swinton did not glance directly toward the Cholla Kid. He leaned farther over the bar to become busily engaged in a loud, innocuous conversation with one of the bartenders. But his bleak eyes were resting on the back mirror.

In that same mirror, Cholla saw the burly man turn from the card players and return unconcernedly to the bar, sidling along it to a place beside him. He felt the pig eyes scanning him from head to foot. Finally he turned his head to look at the man. Scarface's lips writhed in a species of grin, and his tone was apparently meant to be ingratiating.

"Have a dust wash, stranger?" he rumbled, planting a boot on the rail beside Cholla's.

"Don't mind if I do," the cowboy said easily, and his grin was indolently unconcerned. "Kinda long drag down here from where I come from— makes a feller plumb dry."

"Maybe you was in a hurry," said Scarface with a leer. "That's calc'lated to make a jasper some drier."

"Maybe I was," said Cholla thinly. He lifted his drink, tossed it down, swallowed the chaser. "Here's to happy days and a long summer," he nodded.

"Where'd you ride from?" Zach asked abruptly,

setting down his glass. "Ain't never seen you in this town o' Hondo nor this neck o' the woods before. When did you get in?"

Cholla turned, one elbow on the bar, a foot on the rail, and regarded him levelly. "I rode down from the Panhandle," he announced in a voice of calm, "and I got here when I came in through those doors."

"Yeah?" Zach's voice grew brittle, his small eyes snapped warning. "What you doin' in Hondo, anyway, cowboy?"

Cholla snapped shortly: "What do *you* do around here, hombre, besides shoot off your mouth in saloons?"

Zach Dagget's face went purple to the explosive point. His piggish eyes bulged, his chest rose and fell with the sudden anger that engulfed him. Fingers twitching, he hunkered into a semi-crouch.

"Why, damn you, you too-smart ranny!" he bawled. "Talkin' to *me* like that! Put a hitch on your tongue! I'll break you in two!"

Cholla Sutton's body turned to steel wire as his elbows came off the bar. One moment he stood against it, cool and watchful, his eyes on the hands of Scarface—the next he was on Zach Dagget like a leaping jaguar.

Twisting like an outlaw cayuse, Dagget ripped his six-shooter, to which his hand had been sliding when Cholla leaped, clear of the leather.

52

He tried to bring it into play. But the cowboy's right fist flashed up, landing a stunning blow. A choked yell was broken off in Zach's throat as his head snapped back, and in that split second, Cholla had grabbed his gun wrist and twisted.

The gun dropped from the pain-paralyzed fingers as Zach let out a bull roar from lips purple with rage. Then before he could get a breath, the panther-like stranger had the bullying Zach around the waist in a steel-trap grip. With a mighty heave he lifted him and flung him savagely across the poker table near the center of the floor. Players leaped to their feet with startled oaths, scattering. The table crashed over with a thud, smashing bottles and glasses. Falling, rolling chips tinkled and mingled with the sound of quickly shuffling feet and jingling spurs.

Zach rolled over on the floor, trying to scramble up, making a desperate dive for his gun. But before he could reach it, Cholla was upon him like a catamount.

"Didn't have enough, huh?" he panted. "Well, here 'tis!"

In one spraddle-legged swoop he had the downed man in his vise-like arms again, lifting him. There was no sound except the labored panting of the fighting men. Cholla's eyes were only on the doors directly ahead as he kicked aside the overturned table. His grunt sounded like the mighty effort of a straining wrestler as he lifted the scar-faced man—and slammed him straight through the swinging doors.

Another roar was torn from Scarface as he hit the sidewalk hard and rolled over and over. Two men outside, just about to enter, backed hastily out of the way, while Cholla, eyes blazing, squared off, waiting for a renewal of the attack.

Then it was that the Cholla Kid got his first sample taste of what treachery there was in the Comal Basin where no such thing as honor or a fair fight was known. One of the men on the board walk outside flipped his gun to Zach Dagget as the burly man scrambled to his feet. With an animal-like snarl, Zach snatched it and staggered back through the swinging doors. He flung up the Colt and fired the instant he caught sight of Cholla.

The Cholla Kid leaped sideways, but the heavy slug creased him under his half-raised arm, spinning him halfway around. No man in the saloon, though, could have followed the lightning draw he made, firing before a breath could be caught.

And his bullet did no creasing. It went true. Zach Dagget barged back against the wall, howling with pain and anger. His smoking gun thudded to the floor from his shattered right hand. Before he could stoop to retrieve it with his left, Cholla was upon him again like an infuriated spirit of vengeance gone berserk.

His pistol rose and fell—only once—but enough. There was the sickening crash of steel against teeth, and with his vicious yell cut off to an unfinished mumble, Zach Dagget crumpled into a heap at the Cholla Kid's feet and lay still.

Without a glance at the unmoving, silent men in the saloon, Cholla stooped, jerked off Zach's gun-belt and flung it behind him. He gathered up the two pistols on the floor, Zach's own which nobody had attempted to retrieve, and the borrowed one. He broke their cylinders and shook out the cartridges. Calmly he walked across the floor and tossed the gleaming guns, empty, behind the bar. Then he whirled around.

"Who in hell is that sidewinder?" he demanded with abrupt sternness. His eyes shot from man to man like glints of chilled steel.

Nobody answered. Boots shuffled against the floor in the momentary silence; restless sounds. The Cholla Kid laughed shortly, with no hint of lightness. His shoulders lifted a little as he shot inquiring glances around.

"Any argument, then?" he demanded. "Anybody else lookin' for another dose of the same medicine? I'm accommodatin' that way."

Still no answer. The tension was growing, though. It showed plainly on the heavy, unprepossessing faces of the denizens of that saloon, in the slight movement of feet when spurs clicked against the floor.

Cholla noted the stiffness of the men's bodies and the bleak watchfulness of dark, glowering countenances; the proximity of their hands to their gun-belts.

The cowboy was not insensible to the fact that the situation was one of touch and go. His one chance was a continued bravado. Any act of his might precipitate the free-for-all battle for which these *paisanos* were ready. Stranger that he was, he knew he could expect no aid from what cowpunchers were present. They would be neutral, take no sides.

He gave one swift glance toward Sheriff Newt Swinton. That official, still leaning against the bar, made no move, nor said a word. A cold-deck town sure enough.

"All right, then," Cholla said, when he saw no signs of any reply being made. "Have it your own way. Clam up, if you want to. But don't none of you hombres peg me for a greenhorn. I ain't been in hot water for twenty-five years without learnin' some o' the tricks myself."

Calmly holstering his gun, he turned his back deliberately and walked to the door. Right thumb in gun-belt, he turned again there, raking the sullen, silent occupants of the saloon with a stern glance, one that held contempt. Then he shoved open the green swinging doors, flicked a glance up and down the sidewalk, and clomped over to the side of his cayuse. While he was unhitching

Jerky, a man hurried from the saloon, and without a glance at him, trotted down the plaza.

"Lightin' a shuck for the doctor, I reckon," Cholla murmured to the pinto. "Hombre inside shore needs him, Jerky . . . Guess we better be keepin' two eyes wide open in this man's town, or we'll be needin' a couple o' sawbones ourselves—or a nice soft spot on their Boot Hill."

Not glancing at the saloon, nor at the man in search of aid for Scarface, the Cholla Kid reefed his mount and rode away at an easy lope in the other direction.

CHAPTER V

A SINISTER GAME

BEFORE he had gone past a dozen houses, Cholla knew that he was not going to be allowed to ride out of town without being the object of a little attention. Not after such a set-to as that in the Legal Tender.

The man he had left unconscious was not, as was a reasonable guess, the only man in Hondo who would like to know a few things about him—where he had come from, what was his business, and where he was headed. It was a foregone conclusion there were others curious.

A slight, unnoticeable turn of his head as he rode along showed him two men coming out of the saloon. They went to the hitch-rack and got into their saddles.

Taking the same direction Cholla was taking, they rode slowly along. They made no attempt to come up with him. It must be their idea, the cowboy surmised, to give him the impression they had no interest in him. But his lips were grim as he realized that if he rode out of town he must travel unfamiliar trails. He had no more intention now of taking a hand in a game played on strange, dark roads than he had had a few hours previously. Certainly not with men such as these whom he had easily sized up as making it a practice to play only with cards they knew.

The Cholla Kid had started to ride out of town with the intention of sleeping in the open as he was accustomed to do. With men on his trail he changed his mind.

Easing Jerky's slow lope down to a measured jog he went on, giving no indication that he suspected he was being followed. His eyes were searching for a corral or livery barn. There was a low chuckle in his throat at thought of the probable surprise of the men behind him when he rode straight toward the first livery barn in sight. A weather-beaten sign on a tumble-down, rambling frame building apprised him that he had reached the:

SHORTHORN STABLE
Sid Grumbles, Prop.

The two horsemen rode slowly on past as he turned into the stable door. It must upset their calculations a bit, Cholla imagined, to discover that he was not going out of town at all. He was not running away from trouble. He was not running into it, either, which would be likely, if he did leave. If the Cholla Kid had to face any more of Hondo's sweet citizens he preferred to do it in the light of day. Anyway, he figured he would be merely living up to the impression he hoped he had left in the saloon by not lighting a shuck out of town.

A yawning man came out of the tack room as he rode on in. A lantern, wick turned low, burned dimly in the office. Cholla said briskly to the skinny, shifty-eyed fellow who lounged toward him:

"You Grumbles?"

The man's yawn widened, he nodded, and said, "Yep," when his lips came together.

"Turn out your hostler, then," Cholla ordered snappily. "I want water, feed, and a stall. Plenty of the first two, and a clean bed-down for my nag. Savvy the burro?"

"Yep." The livery stable man yawned again, before he said languidly: "Shoot him in Number Six there." He managed to lift his head and let out a bawl: "*Chongito!*" That brought a murmured answer and a sleepy Mexican youth from a straw bunk in the runway. The skinny man barked an order or two and turned the Mex over to Cholla.

The cowboy from the Panhandle saw to it himself that his pinto was being capably taken care of, then he walked back to the tack room with the ferret-faced Grumbles. He paid the stableman in advance. Grumbles unbent a little at that, but his remarks were those to be expected of a resident of Hondo.

61

"Stranger?" he asked, biting off a chew of tobacco.

The Cholla Kid nodded. He meant not to resent anything this man might say. There was no reason for a repetition of what had occurred in the Legal Tender.

"Just down from the Panhandle," he said genially. "Sort o' lookin' the country over, as you might say. Come I should run across an outfit I liked, I might sign on for a while. Know any needin' a first class rider?"

Grumbles shook his head, sizing up Cholla and the guns at his hips.

"Outfits all right filled up about now," he said, scratching his head in thought. "Unless—Well, a man that can sling a gun as well as ride might not be so bad off. . . ."

Cholla laughed and shook his head. "No'me," he said. "Me, I'm not aimin' to shuffle off this life right soon—rather take a chance on nursin' longhorns. Got plenty good times in front o' me yet—" He stopped suddenly, then drawled: "Say, that reminds me . . . I just got in—don't know this town. Where's honkytonk town here? This burg got one?"

"Hell, yes." Grumbles looked at him pityingly. This hombre must be green, his eyes plainly showed him thinking. What kind of places had he ever been in that he couldn't point right to that bright-lighted, noisy section—whatever

62

part of town it happened to be in—the moment he ambled into a town's plaza? But he only advised: "You'll see it a ways from here. Keep walkin' along that street yonder till you come to the Comal. Cross the bridge, an' you're there, pilgrim. This *must* be your first visit to Hondo, huh?"

"You guessed it, pardner," Cholla grinned. "Heard it's some lively place—plenty doin'—I'd like to see." He turned toward the open door, pulling down his hat and swaggering a little. "Much obliged. Reckon I'll amble along and look over the *señoritas* some. See you later."

At the rickety table he stopped, pushed down the lever on the lantern, raised the chimney and touched his freshly made quirly to the flame. He nodded carelessly to Grumbles, then stepped out into the night, swinging away in the direction indicated.

He shot a glance up and down the street. There was no sign of the two men who had started out to follow him. Probably they had returned to the saloon, to wait for a better opportunity. But, though he did not look back, he was perfectly aware that the lantern-jawed stableman was watching him out of sight. And he grinned, knowing that the hatchet-faced gentleman most likely had a more or less bewildered frown on his brows, trying to place Cholla and what was his business in the town of Hondo.

Once gaining the protection of sheltering shadows, he stopped, looking back and waiting for the inquisitive Grumbles to go back inside. When the man finally did decide to continue his sleep, Cholla, in the deep shadows between two buildings, knelt and removed his spurs, stuffing them into a pocket.

Taking advantage of the intense darkness cloaking the unlighted byways, he sought out an isolated *cantina* on the edge of town and bought a flask of whiskey. Even there he knew he was the object of inquiry, and got out as quickly as he could. He refused to accept but one proffered drink, but himself purchased for the nondescript Mexicans and the few men present of the lower type riffraff of the town. He was asked no questions there, for though all strangers in Hondo might be suspect, none of those men were in sufficient authority to take questioning into their own hands.

Back in the street, he went on, sauntering at last boldly into the plaza and making for the ramshackle hotel. The old man in charge, clerk and general factotum, so nearly swallowed his quirly when he looked up from where he was dozing in a chair tipped back against the office wall, that Cholla knew his description had already been broadcast. The old chap had unquestionably had his version of the fight in the Legal Tender across the way, with the information that the fighting stranger had fled town. He saved his quirly, however, by snapping together his tooth-less gums, with a rather surprised look on his face that the stranger had not taken it away from him. He jumped up with alacrity.

"Howdy, stranger," he mumbled affably. "Somethin' I can do for you?"

"Yes," Cholla nodded. "Room for the night—one that's got a pitcher o' water in it . . . Got to wash up."

The quirly quivered as the old fellow hobbled hastily over to the key rack, took down a key, handed it to the cowboy.

"Number Eight, pilgrim," he said, his voice twittery. "You'll find it right down to the end o' the hall one flight up. My rheumatiz—"

Cholla grinned. The old man's desire not to be any longer in the fighting stranger's presence than necessary was obvious.

"Thanks, pop," he said. "I'll find it." He started on toward the stairs. "See you in the morning."

The stranger in Hondo climbed the dim-lighted, rickety stairs without a backward look. He knew without looking that the old clerk was watching every step he made, wondering at his temerity in boldly staying this night in the town where he, a total outsider, had been in a single-handed gun battle, and that there must be men looking for reprisal.

The old man's fixed stare at Cholla's broad

back did not waver until the cowboy was out of sight and he heard his retreating footsteps along the upper hall. Then he jumped as though a gun had been aimed at him as the front door creaked. A man came in off the porch. The ancient clerk crooked a thin old finger at the newcomer, and as the man came near he whispered:

"That jasper that done up Zach Dagget over in the Legal Tender ain't lit a shuck, nohow. He's just gone upstairs—in Number Eight for the night. He's some husky, he is, and if my old eyes ain't lyin' to me he's one bad hombre to fool with. Them steely eyes o' his give me such a turn I danged near chawed up my quirly."

The other man shut his lips tight, and scratched his head.

"Zach's some job for Doc Somers, right now," he demurred. "But I wouldn't be a mite surprised if they wasn't some gents would like right well to know where that fightin' fool's holed in . . . Seems he give the boys the slip at Grumbles' livery barn."

"Yeah," the old man nodded. "Reckon so." Then he winked, as he pulled a key ring from his pocket. "The old man—you know who— warn't maybe such a fool when he put all them newfangled Yale locks on them doors . . . I got the pass key right here."

"Uh-huh." The other fellow winked back as he started for the street door. "Might be some hombres would be wanting to make a little social call before mornin'."

The speaker went out and closed the door. The old clerk, well pleased with his own small bit in helping Hondo, tipped his chair back against the wall and let his eyelids droop.

In Number Eight upstairs, with a bureau pulled up before the door so that he might not be annoyed with unexpected arrivals, the Cholla Kid was busy. By the flickering gleams from a small lamp, he set about giving himself his delayed first aid. From the cracked pitcher he poured the bowl full of water, washed his wounds as carefully as he could. Then he laved them in the raw liquor he had bought at the *cantina*— primitive treatment, but efficient, as he had discovered on more than one occasion.

This completed, he did not continue his undressing. Instead, he got back into his shirt and horsehide coat.

Blowing out the light, he went to the window, pulled aside the curtain to investigate. He nodded, satisfied. Better than he had hoped for. He had thought he might have to drop out of that two-story window by the aid of tied bedding. He was pleased when he saw that the slanting roof of the lean-to in the back came right up to his window. That lay-out might not have been so pleasing under other circumstances.

Cautiously he raised the window to its fullest height and climbed out on the roof, sliding down it to the eaves. He waited a moment there, listening. He was at the rear of the hotel and, hearing no sound, he dropped the short remaining distance to the ground.

There was a low chuckle in the Cholla Kid's throat as he slipped off through the black darkness. If men were to come to the hotel, with the intention of making him a surprise call during the night, theirs would be the surprise. Or the unpleasant shock might be the proprietor's, if his bureau had to be smashed before the room could be entered.

Taking a roundabout course, keeping away from the streets, he made his way back to the livery barn. Sifting through dark alleys he slid near the big back door, approaching it from the rear. Screened by scrubs, he listened for a time. Then he went to the door, softly opened it, and slid inside. He had, on his previous visit, taken the precaution, while hanging up his saddle and blanket, of unlatching the door while Grumbles was not looking.

Re-hasping it, he climbed the ladder leading to the feed loft above. Cautiously striking the match necessary to keep him from making any noise stumbling over unfamiliar territory, he made his way forward to the soft and fragrant haymow. His position was directly above the tack room, and he could hear the raucous snores of the unsuspecting stableman.

Bedding himself down, Cholla prepared to catch a lot of shut-eye. He had no intention of being done out of his night's sleep. He had already paid for it—in a bed, but in another place that was not so safe as this where he was taking fewer chances of being disturbed.

He was sure that he could no more than have drowsed off when a sudden loud knocking on the office door below and a growl of voices outside roused him. Noiselessly sliding from the haymow, he crawled along on his belly to a wide floor crack through which a glimpse of light came dimly. He lay there motionless, listening.

He heard Grumbles get up, growling pro-fanely, and unlock the door. Then he heard two men clump in, shut the door behind them with a bang and come on into the tack room, following the stableman. Somebody turned up the low-turned wick and Cholla could see the newcomers plainly.

"Did that hombre ridin' a paint hoss stable here tonight?" one of them asked without preamble.

"Yep," replied Grumbles. "Hoss is back in Number Six, bedded down. Why? What's up, Crow?"

Instead of answering, the man called Crow snapped back:

"Where's the jasper at?"

Grumbles shook his head. "Dunno. He lit out as soon as he stabled. Headin' toward honkytonk town, he said." He grinned dryly. "The *señoritas* must be a-doin' of their duty. I ain't seen him since."

"Hummph!" The other's tone was disgusted, as he glanced around. "Did he leave his war-bag and his slicker roll here?"

"Yep." Grumbles gestured with a lean, long arm. "Hangin' back there with his kak and blanket. What's goin' on, I asked you, Ben Crow?"

"Plenty." Crow snorted, then with a gesture to the man with him: "Chug," he ordered, "you slide out an' keep an eye open in case he drifts up. Ought to be good and happy by now, at that, if he's acrost the bridge . . . I'll jest have a look through his stuff while he's gone. . . ." He moved toward the tack room. "Bring that lantern, Sid— c'mon."

The man Crow was a scrawny, thin-faced hombre with prominent buck teeth and Adam's apple, and a cast in one eye. Cholla could no longer see him nor the stableman when they passed from the territory covered by the crack by which he lay, but he could hear them plainly. Crow was losing no time in hauling the Cholla Kid's saddle, tarp roll and war-bag from the rack and broaching them in order. Cholla's lips tightened grimly at the indignity, then he grinned. He wished them luck for all they would find.

"What's all this here about, anyhow?" demanded Grumbles, nervously holding the lantern. "What's this jasper done, I'd like to know?"

"Plumb plenty," growled Crow. "More'n plenty for a hombre nobody knows and who can't, or won't give no proper 'count of hisself, or what he's doin' in Hondo whatsoever. Rides in here tonight an' raises billy-be-damned in the Legal Tender. Wipes up the floor with Zach Dagget— lays him out colder'n a frawg."

"Dang my eyes!" The stableman's voice was unbelieving. "Zach Dagget! You don't mean it! Say, that feller must a' been weaned on gall bladder. Where's he come from? You know? Says somethin' to me about the Panhandle, he did, but—"

"Uh-huh—that's his story." Crow's tone was acid. "Panhandle, so he says. Rode in from the Seven-Mile Pass, so some o' the boys report. They seen him jog in. But Newt's been a-talkin' some to Zach while Doc Somers was patchin' him up, and he's been buzzin' with two-three the other boys, and Newt thinks the ranny rode in from the *west* 'stead of east."

"How come?" Grumbles wanted to know, his voice as puzzled as that of any man to whom subtleties are a secret. "Didn't you just say some o' the boys seen him get into town from the east?"

Crow laughed shortly. "Maybe they did—and

71

then maybe again they'll think it over and *know* they was mistook. What they said about seein' this jasper was before they found old man Lynn Merrill a-layin' out in the coulee eight or nine miles 'tween here and the Kuykendall spread—which shore is west from here. He was shot plumb full o' bullet holes."

"*Lynn Merrill? Dead?*" There was no mistaking that information was a real startler for Sid Grumbles, proprietor of the Shorthorn Stable. Cholla could hear the hatchet-faced man's sharp intake of breath.

"Plenty dead," remarked Crow dryly. "Him and his hoss, too. Sheriff's gone out there now—didn't wait for daylight."

"And hell a-poppin' plumb soon," groaned the stableman, as Crow tossed down the Cholla Kid's war-bag in disgust.

Cursing at his failure to unearth damaging evidence, Crow replaced the kak, slicker roll and war-bag on the racks. Again warning Grumbles to secrecy about his visit, he took his departure. Lanky Sid, grumbling unintelligibly, let him out the office door, fastened it after him and went back to bed. In the loft above him, the Cholla Kid was sneaking back to the haymow. But not to sleep—right then. There was too much to think about.

Lying there in the dark, it looked as if he, Ace Sutton, the Cholla Kid, a riding stranger in Comal

Valley, had bought a hand in a sinister game. From what he had heard Crow—unquestionably a deputy sheriff—say that night, somebody was going to try to job him for that Merrill killing. Well, he would have to play the game.

But even as he tried to close his eyes for the sleep he was most likely going to need badly, his eyelids shut down on the picture of a slim, lithe girl in riding clothes, her gold-brown hair making a halo about her piquant face in the lamplight through a doorway, and with blue eyes that had looked at him scornfully. There was a clutch at his heart at the thought that tomorrow there would be only pain and sorrow and tragedy in those blue eyes.

CHAPTER VI
A CONFESSION

CHOLLA'S mental picture of Sanna Merrill's tragedy could not do justice to its poignant reality. All night long, while the range lay under the ghostly light of the stars, in eerie darkness, she sat by the side of her father. He was home at last, but never to speak to her again. As silent as the night she sat there. Now and again a trembling hand went out to touch his icy one. Her lips moved soundlessly as she made her vow never to rest until she had brought to their deserts the killers of the man she had worshipped.

Not a sob broke from her lips. There was no sound anywhere about the ranch, except for the faint stirrings in the shadowy thickets, the mournful hoot of an owl that soared through the night on silent wings; and ever so often the small shuffle of boots on the ranch house porch, or the murmur of a man's husky whisper.

Men were out there, men who had come from nearby ranches as the news raced across the ranges that Lynn Merrill had been brought home bushwhacked. Fighting men who had come to offer their guns and their lives to Sanna Merrill to avenge her father's death, and to give her what rough sympathy they could.

She was grateful for it, but this one last night she wanted to remain alone with her father. The prayers that went up from her heart were intense that she should be shown how to bring vengeance on those who had been responsible for the terrible tragedy.

Whenever there swept over her the full realization of all her loss meant, the pain in her heart was unbearable. Death was so awful in its finality. No matter what was promised of that vague "other time". She could almost hear now the words she would hear in reality the next day when the parson would drone:

"I am the resurrection and the life. Whoso believeth in me . . ."

But even then, she knew, the prayer in her soul would be the same as it was now as she sat alone, tense, tight-lipped, dry-eyed, with a grief too deep for tears:

"God, help me to find them! Help me to make them *pay!*"

The first hint of dawn breaking was in the gray sky before Sanna realized that at last the terrible night had passed. She knew it first when she heard the movements of the men on the porch who had kept vigil with her. Awkwardly they were tiptoeing away to look to the horses. The sound of faint sobbing came from the kitchen where old Maria was cautiously rattling the stove preparatory to getting breakfast.

Life was going on, just like that. But Dad would never be of it again.

Sanna straightened up. Firm purpose was in her eyes. He would not think her his brave, gallant girl he had always believed her to be, if she did not go on with Life. Somehow she *must!* It was up to her to carry on. She was the last of the family now, and she must fight against their enemies as he had always fought. And she must not be afraid.

Afraid? A memory of something he had said to her over and over came to her as if he, lying there so cold and still, had spoken to her.

"You must play the game according to the rules, Sanna, and you must not be afraid."

Her head erect with a new purpose, she got up and went to the window, looking out. The dawn was breaking clear and sweet, with the tang of distant sage brush mingling with that of waving alfalfa and the hint of pine scent sweeping down from the high parapets of the darkly looming Ramireñas. A few stars on the far horizon were bravely fighting not to blink their last, but beyond the farthest hills on the east a growing red and gold smear showed that soon a sun would again be rising to beat down its coppery rays.

Sanna's gaze went to the deep purple of the arroyo which last night she had so futilely watched for her father's return. A deep sigh trembled her body. He was here now; he had come back; it was another day—but would he know it?

Dimly heard from a distant hillside came the mournful wail of a coyote. The answer from another hill accepted the coming of day. The wail's weird echo was in the girl's heart. She shivered once, her hands clenching while her eyes closed in a prayer for strength. Then she turned, and with just one backward glance toward the still figure, went out into the kitchen to begin a new day—a new life, without Lynn Merrill.

Old Maria, fingering her beads, mumbling and sobbing as she worked, stared in open-eyed astonishment when the dry-eyed, tight-lipped girl stood suddenly before her. In her peon way she could not understand a grief that did not expend itself in hysterical emotion. The old woman threw her arms about the girl, her sobs growing to a wail.

"*Chiquita*! Ah, *chiquita*! *Madre di Dios*, what will we do—?"

Gently Sanna loosened the clinging arms. She said calmly, with no sign of her heartbreak in her voice:

"If you will hurry breakfast, Maria? . . . We will be having a number of extra people—some of the ranchmen have stayed all night. . . . We will be leaving the ranch, as soon as we've had coffee,

78

for Hondo. There are some things I must attend to—" She winced at the thought of her errand to town, but her tone was brave. "And I shall need some kind of a black dress—Oh, I know Dad would not want me to—to—But this once, I—I must—"

She glanced up as Kip Helm, her father's foreman, opened the outer kitchen door and came in. He had heard what she said, and started a protest.

"But Miss Sanna, you shorely ain't thinkin' of goin' into Hondo yourself! The boys and me—well, I reckon we can do all the things for the boss that had ought to be done, and—"

Sanna's eyes were sad, but unwet with tears.

"I shall attend to things for—Dad—myself, Kip," she said gently. "He—I'm sure he would wish it so."

So it was that the sun had not skirted the horizon completely when Sanna Merrill, riding her own white-faced black mare, with an escort of grim-faced, heavily-armed men on horseback flanking her, was on the road to Hondo. Behind them—far enough back, at Kip Helm's orders, that she should not hear its mournful rattle—came an empty spring-wagon.

Disdainful of the threats of danger he knew were hanging over him, Cholla Sutton was up and drifting about the town of Hondo long before Sanna Merrill and her retinue reached it. It was

79

no trick at all for him to make his get-away from the Shorthorn Stable that morning. Quite unconscious that he had harbored a guest in his hay loft during the night, Sid Grumbles snored blissfully on while Cholla made his way down the ladder at the first gray of dawn. Nor did Conghito, curled up on his feedbag pallet, stir. His loud, even breathing was not interrupted as Cholla let himself out of the barn's rear door and breathed the early morning air of the open.

Trouble might be ahead in that town for the Cholla Kid, was in his thoughts as he walked away and headed for the town's plaza, but he meant to be ready for it. They would not catch him unawares; nor at all, if he had his way about it. He was determined he would not be driven from the town until he was ready to go.

As the sun tinted the east, he made his way unobtrusively to an out-of-the-way eating place called Hole-in-the-Wall. There he got outside of a substantial and much-needed breakfast.

Few people were in the streets. None of them looked at Cholla with any more than the usual curiosity given any stranger. It was apparent that the population of Hondo did not circulate much by day, the majority of its citizens coming out of their holes for their living only after nightfall. Realizing that his tobacco supply was painfully low, and that he would need more, no matter where he should go when he did drift out of town, Cholla sauntered into Simmons General Store after it.

He was just coming out of the store with his pockets filled with smoking tobacco when he saw three riders draw up before an adobe building on the south side of the plaza. They were two men, and a girl riding a white-faced mare was between them. He recognized her instantly—Sanna Merrill. Her blue eyes were looking straight ahead, her lovely face was pale and set. The two men with her were not hard to place. Cowmen, both of them, weather-bronzed, stern of face, with six-shooters swinging at their hips.

Without appearing to, Cholla watched them from the board sidewalk as the trio of riders dismounted and went into the adobe building. A few minutes later he saw a light spring-wagon drawn by a couple of buckskins enter town from the Encinal road. As it came nearer, he saw that a runty, grim-visaged puncher with cold blue eyes held the reins. He, too, came straight on and drew up before the building into which the three had disappeared. Cholla saw that the place was the local undertaking establishment. He knew then what they had come for—what the spring-wagon would carry back to the ranch. And all the sympathy in his heart went out in a flood to the girl on her saddest of missions.

On impulse Cholla headed toward the building himself. The runty, bow-legged puncher regarded him with suspicious, sombre eyes as he walked idly up to the wagon. Cholla started to speak to the man, but stopped short as the girl emerged from the door and came toward the wagon. The two riders who had entered the place with her stopped in the doorway, speaking to some one behind them.

Sanna Merrill's features were ashen, her lips a taut, hard line, her eyes chill as frost. And Cholla Sutton, looking at her, knew that her grief was deeper and more bitter than all the lament and fury in the world. The sight of her moved him strangely—far more so than he had been the night before when he had first realized that it was this girl's father who had been killed out there in that lonely land without being given a chance.

Dull rage swept through him—rage at the dry-gulching coyotes who had done this thing to her. Always he had acted with the thought, and he did so now. Stepping quickly around the wagon, he came nearer to her just as one of the men in the doorway was approaching, saying to her gently:

"That's all we can do right now, Sanna. Everything'll be 'tended to . . . If you'll just go on and buy what you've got to, we can ride on and Kip here'll be bringing—"

Sanna looked at the man steadily as she said, her tone low:

"Kip can come along with us, Bart. . . . Don't worry about me—it's for Dad."

She turned, and Cholla was standing in front of her, his hat raised. He spoke quickly, ignoring the scowl on the face of the cowboy in the wagon. There was swift, glowering inquiry in the eyes of the other two men as they stopped short on their way to their ground-hitched horses, looking back.

"I heard about your trouble, Miss Sanna," Cholla said soberly, "an' I'm shore sorry. If there's anything I can do to help, anything you want done at all, you can count on me."

She looked up at him, at the straight, sturdy manhood of him with his bronzed face and serious gray eyes. There was a look of inquiry in her own pained blue eyes. Then recollection and recognition came into their dry depths.

"Oh, yes," she said listlessly. Her faintly spasmodic catch of breath, like a sigh long held in and now escaping with her first spoken words, touched him as nothing ever had before. "I remember you now. You were the man who stopped by the ranch after matches last night. Thank you, but I don't suppose there's anything you can do. . . ." Her voice went forlorn. "What is there that anybody can do?"

Cholla's voice lowered as he took one step nearer to say quietly:

"I don't want to appear as if I was curious-like Miss Sanna—I want you to believe that—or I'm not one to come hornin' in at a time like this. But there's somethin' you ought to know about this grievous affair, and looks to me like the sooner you and them that are your real friends knew it the better it would be all around. Could I have a word with you somewhere, sort o' confidential-like?"

Her eyes widened, searched his with feverish intentness.

"You *do* know something then?" Her voice was lower, just above a whisper. "Someway, I thought so last night, but—"

"Yes'm," he said evenly. "I do know some-thin'—now. When I saw you last night, anything I might have told you would only have been a guess."

"I've got to know!" said the girl tensely. "What is it? Tell me!"

Cholla shook his head. "Not here, Miss Sanna. It wouldn't do—not even for me to be seen by—*some*—talkin' to you, and—"

"Then where?" Her eyes were burning flames.

Cholla had already been considering that. He asked her:

"Are you goin' back to the ranch right away?"

"Yes," Sanna nodded. "As soon as I stop by the store for a few minutes . . . And we've got to go over to see the minister."

"*Bueno*," Cholla said quickly. "I've got to get away from here right now. But I'll saddle up my hoss—he's down at the livery barn—and join you on the road outside town *muy pronto*. That okay?"

He gave no indication that he might have trouble keeping that appointment, that there might be a set-to with Grumbles before he could get his pinto, or that there were others who had an interest in keeping him in Hondo. He suggested no "ifs" because he meant to *keep* that appointment. It would take more than a hatchet-faced livery man with a sawed-off shotgun, or a townful of badmen to keep him from telling what he knew, now that his mind was made up. So he only nodded again and walked away when the girl said:

"Yes, that will be all right. We'll be looking for you about twenty minutes out."

CHAPTER VII
THE ROAD CONFERENCE

CHOLLA had less difficulty in getting Jerky than he had thought he might. He did not enter the livery door by the front door but via the back, as he had earlier made his departure. As he went softly toward the tack room, then stared into the office, he saw no sign of Sid Grumbles. The stableman was out for his breakfast, likely. Good!

Making his way back toward his pinto's stall, however, he ran spang into the Mexican, Conghito, and the whites of the dark-skinned Mex's eyes rolled in fright at sight of him. The hostler's mouth dropped open to yell. Plain enough Conghito had not been asleep during that conversation and visit in the night, and he had not been expecting the man the sheriff wanted calmly to march in for his horse.

Cholla stopped the yell from the Mex at its inception, as he made a sudden spring at him, catching him and pinning his arms behind him.

"Not a sound out of you!" he gritted. "I want my hoss and I'm goin' to get him. You keep your mouth shut and you'll not be hurt."

The Mexican was obediently mum, but Cholla

saw to it that he should remain that way for a time, at least. He slid a bandanna into Conghito's mouth after he had quickly tied the man with some harness lines, fastening him to a stall. He said, walking away toward Jerky's stall:

"Too bad, *hombrito*, but I had to do that. Grumbles will be back soon, I reckon, and you can yell your head off then. Tell 'em, if they want to know, that I'll be lopin' for the Ramireñas by then."

Quickly he threw his saddle across the pinto's back as Jerky nosed him, whinnying a small welcome. With slicker roll and riata in place, he rode out of the barn.

There were more people abroad by now, and when Cholla jogged out of town, compelled to pass the plaza for the Encinal road, he felt curious eyes upon him from men in stores and on sidewalks. His lips tightened. Didn't take long in that cold-deck town for news to get around. But if he could get a head start, before that sheriff acted on general principles and the urging of Zach Dagget, he could show Jerky's heels to all of them. In the meantime, there was something else he wanted to do.

As he reached the outskirts of the town, he increased Jerky's pace to a jog trot, and a little further along broke into a lope. Presently, after he had been riding ten minutes or more, he made out the spring-wagon he had seen. It was going slowly on, not more than half a mile ahead. The three on horseback were riding just ahead of it.

When he caught up with them, the whole cavalcade halted, the stern men looking at him questioningly, as they all drew up at the side of the road, but saying nothing. Sanna, herself looking inquiringly at Cholla Sutton, was the first to speak.

"Whatever you have to say," she said evenly, indicating the trio with her by a slight gesture, "you can say before these men. They are Bart Lacey of the L Open L, and Jeff Kuykendall of the Bay Lazy 3 Slash. Neighbors. Friends of mine—and of my father's. And here—" she kept her eyes away from the spring-wagon as she motioned toward the man driving it—"is Kip Helm. The Rafter M foreman. He was my father's trusted friend for years." She glanced again at Cholla. "And your name is—? I've forgotten. Sorry."

"Sutton, ma'am," Cholla said soberly. "Ace Sutton." He nodded from one to the other of the escort. "Proud to know you men . . . Thanks for waitin' for me like this, and I won't keep you long. I'll get right down to cases. What I've got to tell you that you ought to know, I'm thinkin', is this—"

Without more ado, as briefly but as explicitly as he could, he recounted his experiences of the previous night, starting with the man he had seen on the rock ledge above the spring—the man who had so mysteriously disappeared. He graphically told of the mêlée on the trail and of his finding the body of the grizzly-haired man and the injured horse. He recounted the adventure of the men firing on him in the barranca and of his escape from them. He told of stopping by the ranch and how his instinct, prompted by something in Sanna Merrill's manner, told him she might be waiting for the very man who had been foully murdered in the coulee. He got quickly then to his run-in with Zach Dagget, and his vague suspicion, now, that the burly Zach might have been the man he had seen on the ledge. Finally he told them of the search of his kak and war-bag in the stable, and of Ben Crow's conversation with Sid Grumbles.

"And that's the lay-out, folks," Cholla finished quietly. "I don't believe there's anything I've forgot to tell you. I'm a stranger hereabouts, and none of you know me from Adam's off ox, but it shore looks like I'd been dealt a hand in this game, whether I craved to sit in or not. I'd be plumb proud to chunk in with you folks, though, case you could use me. 'Course I realize you don't know the first thing about me, and I ain't claimin' to be no saint, but I've got no more use for a bushin' drygulcher than you have. If somebody's aimin' to job me for this killin', like that deputy, Crow, hinted, why I ain't aimin' to take it layin' down. And—" he shot a single quick glance at Sanna—"it might be that I could be of a little help when it comes to runnin' down the real gulchers and makin' them pay."

"You don't know Hondo and the Basin, cowboy," put in Lacey, bitterly, his head shaking dolefully. "There's things goin' on here that'd make the devil ashamed of hisself. If you've got any sense whatsoever, now that you're out of the town, you'll head out an' keep ridin'. Stayin' here means bad trouble for you—likely the same end that come to Lynn Merrill, as square a cowman as ever owned a brand. Or maybe worse. Folks on the level are best off lightin' a shuck away from here."

"I told him that last night," Sanna said, her tone low, despairing. "When—when I thought maybe he might be coming into the Basin as another hired gun."

"And I told you I wasn't," Cholla said quickly. "No'me. I've done plenty things in my time, maybe, but I've never hired out as a killer. My guns ain't for sale, but I'm plumb willin' to use 'em, free and plenty, if needs be."

Jeff Kuykendall said, after he had been sizing up Cholla quietly:

"You say your name is Suttin, huh? And you was tellin' Sanna you come from New Mex?"

Cholla eyed the rancher evenly, weighing an idea. Then he decided to lay his cards face-up

91

on the table. His instinct told him he could trust these men; that he could go a lot farther and fare much worse than with them as his friends, trusting him in return.

"Sutton, yes," he said slowly. "But maybe there's a little somethin' else that you ought to know about me. Just between us five and the buckskins, I'm better known west of the Pecos and in the Rincon country as the Cholla Kid—if that means anything to you. I told you I wasn't no saint, but I haven't seen any sheriff's dodgers of my likeness this side o' Mobeetie, so I reckon that coyote who totes a star and gun in Hondo don't know anything about me yet . . . Hasn't got me placed, as you might say. I might get in some right good licks before he does."

Four pairs of eyes, surprise and uncertainty in their depths, were boring into him. Lacey let out a gusty breath; Kuykendall grunted; Kip Helm made no sound, but his features grew frosty. Only Sanna Merrill sat her horse regarding him with puzzled eyes. She was the first to make a comment.

"I've never heard of any Cholla Kid," she said finally. "Terrible or otherwise. So you can't be so notorious, or the story of your misdeeds would certainly have reached this far. Anyway, I—I don't believe you would shoot anybody in the back—so that you could rob them."

"No'me," said Cholla, the ghost of a wry smile

92

edging his mouth. Then there was a touch of anxious pleading to be believed as he looked at the girl and added; "And now, Miss Sanna, seein' as we're all bein' kind o' confidential-like and you've seen all my cards, won't you give me a little more information—so's I won't be shootin' in the dark? You just said somethin' I didn't guess before—a little different from most dry-gulchin's. You say your dad was robbed?"

Sanna looked from Lacey to Kuykendall, with a side glance for Kip Helm, then back to Cholla, her weary eyes on him steadily.

"Yes," she said, in a tone that led the Cholla Kid to believe she meant to trust him in return, "he was robbed. No one but Bart Lacey here, Kuykendall, Kip and myself—at least that was what we believed—knew that Dad went to San Saba five days ago to arrange for a loan through an old friend there. And was expected back last night. We had no idea anyone could have guessed it, but somebody must have been looking for him, and—"

"Must have been on the lookout for him for some time, too," put in Lacey soberly, "and pickin' out the places to hold him up. Seems like it from what Sutton tell us about a man bein' on the ledge above the spring that there was one feller on the lookout . . . A likely place for a man ridin' a long way to stop—the only spring thereabouts in miles."

Cholla nodded. He knew that. He, too, had looked for water.

"Yeah," nodded Kuykendall, in his characteristically slow way of thinking long before speaking: "Zach Dagget—and I'm a-bettin' it was Zach—saw Sutton restin' up there. He didn't know who he was in the dark, whether he was stranger or no, and so he lights off to let the murderin' rattlesnakes know to pick another spot."

That sounded reasonable to Cholla. He wished there had been a bit of moonlight when he had seen those three heads looking down at him in the barranca. But there was no time now to discuss that phase; there were more important matters, and time was pressing. It would not do to linger too long in that road. So he said to Sanna:

"You were sayin' that your dad went to get a loan? You reckon he got it, huh?"

"I'm sure he did," she said steadily. "We have more reason to know so, now. When he went to San Saba he was to bring back between five and six thousand dollars to pay a mortgage due in three days from now on a section of ranch land, and another mortgage on stock and the home ranch, due in six months. We thought the five of us, including Dad, were the only ones who knew anything about his arrangement in San Saba to raise the money. But somebody else evidently

94

knew—" her tone grew bitter—"and acted on their information."

"I *sabe*," said Cholla, slowly, curling a cigarette. "Who are these mortgages due to, Miss Sanna? Both to the same concern?"

She nodded, drooping a little in her saddle. With that spring wagon so near and its tarpaulin-covered reminder of her tragedy, such things as money and mortgages seemed of little consequence. But she could see Cholla's viewpoint, realized that he must have information if he was to be of any assistance to her and her neighbors in running down the robber and murderer of her father.

"Both to the same, Mr. Sutton," she told him. "To the Stockmen's Bank of Hondo. Mr. Lacey or Kip can give you more details about those loans than I can, probably. But I do know that this will mean a loss that would have broken Dad's heart—the loss of something for which he had struggled and fought a long, long time. They had never been able to down him, but now they will be able to take the Twin Springs section, his pride, away from me right away."

"Won't the bank renew the mortgage?" queried Cholla, eyeing the red tip of his brownie. He was doing some rapid thinking, and some things were coming into his mind so nearly clairvoyantly that it would have astonished the others.

"Hardly," Sanna answered him bitterly. "There's

a man—if you want to call him that—named Boyce Puryear who has been trying to get the Twin Springs section for eight months. He has done everything he could to get it. He made life hell for Dad—Oh, I suppose I shouldn't make an accusation like that, but everybody knows, though they're afraid to say so, that Boyce Puryear is behind so much of the trouble all the real ranchers in the Comal Basin have been up against for some time!" She hesitated, biting her lips as if she feared she had said too much, then went on: "You can imagine how much chance I would have getting any mortgage renewed when I tell you that Puryear owns controlling interest in the bank, and Luke Brundett, the president, is just his dummy catspaw, as coyote-crooked as Puryear himself." She sighed, and her lips trembled, as she flung out her hands. "Well, they were determined to have it—they've got it now! Oh, Dad, Dad!"

For a moment it looked as if she might break down at last, but suddenly she threw up her head proudly, shaking it as though to shake off her own momentary weakness.

"But I'll die, too, keeping the home ranch from those devils!" she said between set teeth.

Cholla Sutton hated further to question her just then, but it had to be. So he asked her, without any sign of the emotion he had felt at seeing her suffering:

"This Puryear you're talking about—who's he, and what's his layout here? Anything except bein' president of the bank?"

It was Kuykendall who answered him, giving Sanna time to regain her composure.

"You're provin' you're a stranger hereabouts, askin' about Boyce Puryear, cowboy," he remarked a little acidly. "He's an hombre who manipulates Hondo's law to suit his own needs, an' he's virtual czar of all Comal Basin. Hard to tell how he got that way, but everything's to his hand. He's district cattle buyer, owner o' the K Breechin' K spread, an' he's got his finger in pretty near every business in town— yes an' plenty outside o' it. Owns the Legal Tender, biggest saloon in Hondo, with one o' his hellions runnin' it, an' he's been mighty damned busy for more'n a year now workin' out a slick plan to grab himself more'n a hundred square miles of prime grassland and water—a regular kingdom."

Cholla had suspected as much. It was the old story of the West, ever new to men who stepped in and let greed run away with them, of trying to get by foul means where fair would not suffice, a territory that would make them kings, with men on a thousand hills and ranges pandering to their vanity.

Lacey nodded, as he put in his oar to complete Kuykendall's information. "Yeah," he added

97

bitterly, so bitterly that it was plain he, too, was one of Puryear's victims, "Puryear's aimin' to be king o' Comal Valley all right. By underhand work—the same old thing regular people can't fight against too long—brand blottin' and fence rustlin', if you ask me. Not to mention foreclosin' on mortgages right an' left at the slightest chance, an' grabbin' water rights."

"Quite a feller," drawled Cholla. "Heard o' his kind before—plenty." He drew a deep breath and tossed away his quirly butt. "Well, I'm kind o' gettin' the drift o' things hereabouts, anyway, folks, thanks to your confidence. . . ." He hesitated a full moment looking at the girl before he asked, slowly: "I s'pose you'll be havin' your dad's funeral today, Miss Sanna?"

"Late this evening," she said steadily. "Out at the ranch."

"Uh-huh." He looked away, feeling awkward, uneasy, in the face of the gallant way the girl took her grief. In his heart was again a blistering rage against the devils who had brought it on her. He said, as he started to turn his horse: "Well, I won't be pesterin' you all any more today—and I reckon you'll be needin' some rest for a few days—"

Sanna said with quick, determined spirit:

"There will be no rest for me, Ace Sutton—ever!—until I find who killed my father! Think I'd want to stop for a minute when each one might count in running them to earth? We've *got* to do something right away!"

Cholla's face brightened with admiration for her spirit.

"Right you are, Miss Sanna. My sentiments exactly. Let's see now—tomorrow is Saturday. I'd like to have a talk with you and these friends of yours some time in the mornin', if it'd be satisfactory to you? Will your place be all right? I've got a sort of scheme up my sleeve where maybeso we can turn the ace in this game, and save that Twin Springs ranch section of yours you were talkin' about."

The quartet looked at Cholla quizzically, but there was a dawning hope in the girl's eyes that the New Mex rider did not miss. She spoke her mind at once.

"I like and trust you, Ace Sutton, Cholla Kid as you call yourself," she said impulsively, her blue eyes squarely upon him. "Something tells me I can, and I'm sure I'm not wrong. But you have no business mixing in our valley troubles. It will only tag you for grief, and perhaps you may have enough of your own. I—we—shouldn't allow you to get embroiled any more than you are now—and that's enough that you ought to start this minute and not stop running your horse until you get beyond the Ramireñas."

Cholla gave her back steady glance for steady glance.

"I bought a hand in this game in Comal Basin last night," he told her tersely. "It's not played out yet, and neither you nor your dad had anything to do with dealin' the cards. But who *is* dealin' is liable to find an extra joker in the deck." He smiled dryly. "Don't you worry about me, Miss Sanna. I'm here because I want to be here, an' I've been takin' right good care of myself for twenty-five years. Trouble and me are not exactly strangers."

Bart Lacey stuck out his hand as he moved his horse to grip Cholla's hand.

"Spoke hawg-tight, hoss high, an' bull strong!" he exclaimed, nodding approbation. "I'm plumb proud to know you, Sutton."

"An' me," echoed Kuykendall, as a rumble in Kip Helm's throat spoke for the foreman. "You're offerin' us your help, an' you shore can count on us up and down, crossways, slaunchways, or any damn way at all. We ain't no friends o' Boyce Puryear. And we aim to make whoever gulched Lynn Merrill do a jig in hell *mucho pronto!*"

"*Mucho pronto!*" echoed the Rafter M foreman fervently.

To Sanna Merrill came the first real expression of her deep emotion she had shown.

"Cholla," she cried with sudden passion, "I, my ranch, my four men—*everything* I have or possess or ever hope to have is yours to use as you see fit, to do with as you please, if only you

100

can bring the killers of my father to judgment! Somehow, I trust you! I have a feeling you may have been sent to me in this awful hour! Come to the ranch, of course—we'll be looking for you in the morning, anytime."

Before Cholla, speechless for a moment at the extravagance of her tense words, could answer, Kip Helm, who was squinting back along the Hondo road, leaped to his feet, blurting out:

"Big covey o' riders comin' a-hellin' this way! Fifteen, twenty of 'em—maybe more!"

CHAPTER VIII

"WE GOT THE DEADWOOD ON HIM"

SANNA MERRILL cried out once in alarm at Kip Helm's warning shout, then sat her horse deadly still, Cholla tensed in his saddle as the rumble of swift-moving horses came to his ears. His sixth sense was again buzzing, every nerve warning him of greater danger than his common sense had already let him know he might expect.

Jeff Kuykendall whirled his horse around to cross the road. He jerked out a sharp word of advice.

"Better ride, Sutton, and fast! Them hombres mean business, and they're shore bad—liable to do anything when they get on the prod."

"Yeah, ride!" urged Bart Lacey, backing his own mount into the road. "We boys can hold 'em here to give you a fair start! Streak it for the Ramireñas!"

Cholla did not answer in words. With thin lips and narrowed eyes, he swiftly unbuttoned his shirt, thrust in his hands and brought them out holding a chamois money belt.

Quickly he tossed it onto the pommel of

Sanna's saddle. She caught it deftly as Cholla shot out some terse instructions.

"Hide that, *pronto*," he urged swiftly. "These jiggers are after my scalp shore as you're born. . . . Maybe about Zach Dagget, and maybe because they've been puttin' two and two together, and even if they can't pin the killin' on me, they figure I know too much. Best thing I can do right now is not to run away, but stay an' see just what their game is." He wheeled toward the two cowmen. "Keep in touch with me, you men, whatever comes up, an' you, Miss Sanna—" he jerked his head around to say to the girl—"you cache that belt o' mine. There's a little over eleven hundred *pesos* in there."

"Why, I don't understand why you want me—" Sanna began uncertainly. A swift glance from Cholla cut off her words and made her hide the belt quickly inside her blouse before the first of the oncoming riders galloped close enough to see any movements in the little group at the side of the road.

The plunging horsemen were very close now, racing in a cloud of dust. Cholla could make out Sheriff Newt Swinton and the squat deputy who had visited the livery barn the night before. They were in the van of the party. A third man whom the cowboy had never seen before was racing along beside them. Some fifteen or eighteen other horsemen drummed hard behind.

"Shore looks like trouble for you, Sutton," Lacey grunted. "You should a' lit a shuck when you had the chance. That's Putt Ratliff with Newt Swinton and Crow—he's Puryear's foreman on the K Breechin' K. Reckon Puryear's on the prod because you put his straw boss, Zach Dagget, on the shelf last night. . . . Anyways, that's good enough reason, 'specially if Dagget knows anything 'bout this dry-gulchin' . . . Which I'm thinkin' he does."

"Yeah," growled Jeff Kuykendall, "Puryear'd do it all right. He's got the sheriff an' the county attorney and hell knows who else under his thumb. . . . Well, we'll be keepin' in touch with you, cowboy, and if this is a frame-up, you can shore count on us."

Long-silent Kip Helm added his grim-lipped monosyllabic comment to that.

"Shore can."

"I'm figurin' it's a frame-up all right," Cholla said thinly, and added his last few hurried remarks before the riders were upon them: "Just remember my name's Ace Renfrow from now on, 'stead of Sutton. And I hail from the Panhandle—knew Mr. Merrill a long time and maybe Miss Sanna. Forget all about the Cholla Kid."

Before anyone could reply, the riders came boiling up, drawing rein so sharply that their horses' hoofs shot up dust and gravel. Snorting, pawing the road into clouds of dust, the posse

105

circled the wagon, paying no attention to its pathetic contents, intent only on the three mounted men. They ignored Sanna Merrill. Rifles and pistols gleamed in the morning sunlight, all of them covering Cholla, who sat with his hands on his saddle horn, shifted sidewise a little, weight in one stirrup. He was more than calm and unflurried—he was deadly cold.

"What's the big idea, Swinton?" snapped Lacey, eyeing the sheriff ominously. "Seems as if you'd ought to be able to see what kind of mission we're on this mornin', and not come bargin' up like this."

Jeff Kuykendall said nothing as he sat slouched in his saddle, but he had a hand hooked near his six-shooter as his eyes ranged coldly over the group of horsemen.

Before the slow-witted sheriff could frame a reply, it was Putt Ratliff, foreman of Puryear's K Breeching K spread who replied sharply and brutally, after only one contemptuous glance at the wagon and its tarpaulin. That look gave notice that he considered the mission of the cowmen of small importance compared with his own. Weather-pitted face drawn into cruel lines, eyes narrowed to slits, he sat his horse, glaring belligerently.

"What's the idea?" he repeated with a snarl. "There's plenty idea, and if you knew this rattlesnake like we know him you wouldn't be settin' here in the road a-talkin' friendly to him—you'd be scotchin' him! Idea?" His snarl became an ominous growl. "Why, this lousy saddle tramp comes skulkin' into Hondo last night makin' out he's plenty salty. Bungs up Zach Dagget by a lot o' rotten tricks, the murderin' skunk! Method in that kind o' madness, oh yeah! Tryin' to cover his tracks, that's what he was thinkin' he was doin', yeah!" He yanked his head around to glare in Sanna's direction. She had moved her horse up to stand protectively beside her father's covered casket. Ratliff's gleaming gun shook menacingly at the Cholla Kid. "*He's* the coyote, Miss Merrill, who killed and robbed your poor paw last night. *Robbed* him, I say, which same maybe you didn't know. No dry-gulchin' about it! Plain ornery hold-up, that's what it was! *And we got the deadwood on this poison, killin' vinagaroon!*"

Sanna gasped, her eyes, newly filled with pain, going from one to the other, from Cholla back to his accusers. She found her voice.

"What do you mean?" she cried desperately. "I don't understand!"

" 'Course you don't!" grated Ratliff, his red-flecked eyes ferociously condemning the icily silent Cholla. "But this killin' hombre was caught red-handed in that coulee where your paw was done for. Three punchers come up with him, standin' over Lynn Merrill's dead body.

107

They'd heard the shootin' and went to investigate. They've been to Hondo to tell their story to Sheriff Newt here, and there ain't no mistakin' it, from their description o' this jasper's looks and his boss that he's the one they seen. Got a damn good look at him, too, they did—chased him for a couple o' hours, in fact, 'fore he somehow managed to give 'em the slip." He turned from Sanna, wheeling his horse, gun up again, levelled at Cholla. "Git offa that hoss, you!" he snarled, foam flecking his lips in his rage.

Sanna's hands were gripping her saddle horn, and her lips were tightly compressed to keep her from crying out. But something was warning her not to speak. Putt Ratliff, in his desire to condemn the Cholla Kid in her eyes and before Bart Lacey, Kuykendall and Kip, had said just a little too much. It fitted in with what Cholla had said, but—Cholla's story had been told first. It bore too much of truth. Under no circumstances, though, must she let these Hondo men guess her thoughts.

With a score of weapons trained upon him, Cholla knew that any show of resistance would be futile. It might be worse, for if Sanna Merrill's range neighbors should come to his defense, they, too, would have no show on earth. He, or Lacey, Kuykendall or the foreman might get one or two of the posse, even more, in a fight, but a swarm of bullets would quickly put an end to battle.

They would be beaten by overwhelming numbers before they had fairly started.

Deliberately he got from Jerky's back in obedience to Ratliff's orders. As he dismounted, two men came toward him, whipping lengths of pigging string from their belts. A trio of others sidled up from behind, weapons cocked and levelled upon his back. Cholla, his face grim and set, flicked a look at the sheriff.

"So I'm a murderer, huh?" he drawled. "I noticed you wasn't so particular last night when it might a' been me who was up on the carpet to be murdered."

"None o' your lip, feller," snapped Swinton, his fish eyes narrowed. He turned and spat through his walrus mustache into the dust at Cholla's feet. "You just get this, an' get it good! Nobody can come murderin' an' robbin' in my county, not so long as I wear a gun an' a star. Thought you 'peared kind o' cocky last night, with all that fist-an'-blood slingin' against Zach—usin' plumb nasty tricks, too. Hummph! T'wouldn't a' been any murder a-tall if he'd done for you."

"No?" said Cholla. There was a queer twist to his thinned lips, but the sheriff did not notice. He had turned to Sanna Merrill and the three silent men ranged alongside her.

"Maybe you think we don't know what we're talkin' about, nohow," he remarked, and there was a tone of triumph in his voice. "Us talkin'

109

about robbery. But 'twas plain highway robbery! We done found the money where he cached it! Now what do you think o' that?"

"Sure about that?" drawled Jeff Kuykendall. "How do you know?"

"Yeah, s'pose you did find some money—how's that to prove it ever was Lynn Merrill's, or that this jasper took it off him?" Bart Lacey wanted to know.

Sheriff Newt was prepared for that, with a lesson well learned. His huge shoulders shrugged.

" 'Cause he ain't nowise so smart as he thinks he is, that's why . . . Five thousand dollars of it in greenbacks and yellabacks, that's what we found. Right where he'd hid it in a mattress in the room in the hotel in Hondo where he pretended he'd holed in for the night. But he didn't want to be where somebody could come an' ask him questions—not last night. Thought he was right smart, but old man Phillips, the clerk, seen him a-sneakin' out the winda just a little while after he'd come in the place. The old feller thought that was kinda funny, so he calls me, *sabe*, and when we look around the room a little, there she is! The whole five thousand! Figured he could sneak back an' get it, this hombre did, when all the shoutin' about Merrill's killin' was over. *And*"—his voice was triumphant as he exploded what he thought was his bombshell—"we *knew* it had been took off Lynn Merrill, 'cause right in the middle o' the wad o' bills, kind o' stuck, so's this hombre hadn't seen it in a hurry, was the note Merrill had made out for the loan!"

The thin smile still on his lips, Cholla looked at Sanna Merrill. Their eyes met. She looked at him sombrely, intently. She was deathly white beneath the shadow of her wide Stetson; her hands were clenched tightly on her saddle pommel. Something passed electrically between them, something that no man in the crowd saw, but it put fresh courage in the Cholla Kid, made him want to fight the world right then and there.

Cholla took one step backward, his jaw muscles tensing as the men with the pigging strings reached him. But the trio seized him suddenly and roughly. A hand was raised then and a pistol barrel smashed with stunning force on Cholla's hatted head. And deaf to the wild screams of terror that burst from Sanna Merrill's lips, the Cholla Kid went down.

Expert hands that could truss up a steer in a few seconds grabbed him. They soon had the unconscious cowboy roped in the pinto's saddle, limp as a sack of oats. With grunts of approval the possemen began to mount. Bart Lacey rode his horse away from the side of the spring-wagon and held up his hand as he stopped before the ring of mounted men.

"Jest a minute," he said quietly. "That feller's gettin' a trial, *sabe*? You may have all the

111

evidence you say you have, but that don't mean no dancin' at the end of a rope. He's gettin' a trial, and me'n Kuykendall are ridin' back to Hondo with you—jest in case."

"Hell!" spat the sheriff of Comal. "He'll git a trial all right. Who was sayin' anythin' different? I'm representin' the law, ain't I? He can lie his head off in court, for all I care. We got the goods on him, Bart, an' you'll shore see we have." He gathered up his reins and gave the sign to his men to be ready to start. "Damn it, I ain't got time to palaver here all day. All set, fellers?" he yelled.

A rumbled growl so assured him.

"Let's go!"

They moved off slowly, gathering speed to a jog trot. Left alone, with only Kip Helm, beside the wagon which held her father's casket, Sanna Merrill, watching the horsemen disappear in a cloud of dust, shuddered, her finger-nails digging into her palms. And in her heart was a prayer.

"Save him, God! For Dad's sake! *Let* him be the man who'll show me who did this terrible thing!"

Her eyes were hot, but dry and weary when she turned to Kip Helm, silently awaiting her command.

"We'd better be going, Kip," she said calmly. "Dad will be—waiting."

CHAPTER IX
FRAMED—AND CAPTIVE

CHOLLA SUTTON (Ace Renfrow to his captors, as Bart Lacey and Kuykendall had explained on the way back to Hondo) came slowly from the shadowy depths of blackness into which he had been pitched when a gun blow had crashed on his head with the roar of a bursting dam. He did not know where he was, how he had got there. On his first faint awakening he seemed floating in space.

His body felt unbelievably weak, as if his veins were filled with water. He did not want to move, was vaguely conscious of a numbness that kept him lying supine, quiet. His brain was numb, too, except that he did realize there was a pain in his head that seemed to fill the world. And the battery of bells that were ringing in his ears was of no great help to him.

A girl's face, with pained, anxious eyes, blue eyes like a summer sky, kept floating before him. Who was she? He tried to remember that, along with why he was feeling so useless. The attempt brought a sound from his lips that must have been a groan, for it roused him more completely.

He did not open his eyes, for they felt too heavy for him to make the effort, but behind his closed lids there passed a jumbled panorama—with the girl again, questioning and frightened. He was groping to remember words of hers he had heard. Or was it a scream, or short, dry sobs that had been cut off with the crash that had sent him into blackness?

The memory of the fear and the aching hurt in those blue eyes was like a dash of ice water in the face of the man lying on the cot in a narrow cell of Hondo's jail. The blood raced through his veins, and his thoughts began to be arrayed in sane alignment.

What had they further made her go through with while he was shut off from the world in that black tomb of unconsciousness? What was she suffering now, out at that ranch with her dead father whom the Cholla Kid had been accused of killing? Surely she could not believe that! Her eyes had not been accusing when he had given her that last steady look. She had seemed to understand. And those weathered cowmen friends of hers had wanted to protect him—he remembered that.

He sat up, holding his head in his hands, his eyes blinking as he looked around. Jail, all right.

He heard voices outside, from the sheriff's office, he judged, and recognized the nasal twang of Sheriff Newt Swinton. The sheriff of

Comal County was protesting, and a rough voice, strange to the cowboy, was saying:

"I tell you you got to watch out, Newt! The old man wouldn't never forgive you if there was any kind of a slip-up. This feller we hauled back here is a killer, *sabe*, make no mistake about that. This gent is good with a smoke-stick, I say, and I pick 'em close. Once you'd give him any kind of chance to get one in his fist, and it'd be pearly gates."

Cholla grinned grimly, wondering who it was that had sized him up so accurately as far as his shooting was concerned. As for the killer part— well, all off on that, unless of course it should happen he could somehow get a chance at a few rattlers who were nesting up in the Comal Basin.

The sheriff was snarling: "Yeah, reckon you're right so far as you go, and he'd as lief chisel a notch on his gun as swaller an *enchillada*, but he ain't goin' to get no chance—no'him. Them pearly gates may be a-swingin' open, but it's *him* that's a-feelin' the draught."

"Wonder just who he is, anyhow?" the other raspy voice was drawling. "Never heard o' any Ace Renfrow, and times I wasn't such a stranger to the Panhandle."

"Ain't goin' to be no Renfrow right *pronto*," the sheriff growled. "The old man's goin' to see to that. This Renfrow'll be dancin' at the end of a riata, sure as guns. Zach's right certain o' him bein' the hombre he saw at the spring, and that bein' the case—"

He did not finish, nor was there need for it, as far as the Cholla Kid was concerned. Framed! Just as he had known he would be. From where he sat, it did not look so good. What Kuykendall and Lacey might do, he had no idea, for naturally he did not know the men had insisted on coming back to Hondo with him to see that he had a square deal. He groaned again, as his hands gripped his aching head, hoping that some plan would come to him. The next words of the men in the office offered him none, but they did have the effect of turning his despair to rage.

"Reckon there's anything in his knowin' Lynn Merrill before?" Sheriff Newt was asking. "Jeff Kuykendall sort o' give a hint like that when he said a man wasn't waylayin' and murderin' his own friends."

"No tellin'," was the reply of the other unseen conversationalist. "Wouldn't surprise me none if he was on his way over this here neck o' the woods to kind a' shine up to the Merrill gal . . . Didn't you catch a couple looks between them out there on the road? Not like plumb strangers, if you ask me."

"He ain't give no 'count of hisself why he's here," mused the sheriff. "Less'n he's hidin' out or somethin', you might be right at that, and if it's so, howlin' wildcats, but won't the old man like *that!*"

Newt Swinton laughed, and on his cell cot Cholla glowered. Something else. Who did he mean by the "old man," and what did Sanna Merrill have to do with him? The next words of the other informed him, in a way. For the rough voice was remarking dryly:

"Just between you and me and the sidewalk, Newt, I'm thinkin' maybe for once the old man has bit off more'n he can chaw. Boyce Puryear may be a man who can have his way all through this Comal Basin, but when it comes to makin' one blue-eyed female see things his way, that's somethin' else again. Sanna Merrill's done told him that—plenty."

"Yeah," snarled the sheriff, "but when her cowboy friend's been swung up for murderin' her dad, and Puryear's got his fists on all her prop'ty, she may be seein' a great big light. Women's like that . . . You mark my words, 'twon't be long before Boyce Puryear's full owner o' Twin Springs and then it'll be the Rafter M ranch, and he'll git the gal"

"Maybe," said the other man, but he did not seem so certain.

Cholla, gritting his teeth because he could not hurl himself on the gossipers, gained the impression that this second man, whoever he was, gauged Sanna Merrill more accurately than

117

did the sheriff. The Cholla Kid had seen her only twice himself, but he was certain she was no girl to be coerced. His blood fairly boiled at his inability to burst through the barred door and take a hand in things right then and there, but there came a sudden interruption from outside that kept him silent. Another voice called out, apparently from a man who stuck his head in the door:

"Rattle your hocks, Sheriff. You're wanted over to the Legal Tender—Puryear's there, wantin' to have a confab."

Cholla heard the jingle of spurs on the bare floor and the scuffle of chairs as two men got up.

"Yeah," came Swinton's drawl. "Comin'. Let's go."

Inside the cell Cholla fell back on the cot and closed his eyes as he heard footsteps crossing to the barred door. He could hear Swinton's breathing as he looked in at the prisoner, then his short laugh.

"Out like a sack o' meal," he chortled. "Zeb Newell shore done a good job with his gun butt. This hombre'll be sleepin' plenty much longer. . . . Come on, Wiz—Ben Crow'll keep an eye on this hombre *mucha pronto*—you can have a little dust wash whilst I'm gabbin' with the boss. Must be right dry after your ride over from the K Breechin' K."

Hearing that, Cholla at least knew something. He heard the men clomp away. Whoever the sheriff had been talking to was from Puryear's ranch, and his name was Wiz. He wished he had had a chance to see the man's face, but probably that would have done him no good.

It looked like one Cholla Kid was in a tight spot any way you took it. That the conference to which the sheriff had been called was for the purpose of tightening up the links in his framing Cholla was sure. He needed no look-in on the men Newt Swinton met to confirm that.

In the private room behind the bar of the Legal Tender, three men sat talking in subdued tones, awaiting the sheriff's arrival. The window shades were drawn, and little light flickered across their faces. One of them, obviously the most important, braced himself in his chair, growling out a "Come in," as there came a light knock on the closed door.

Sheriff Newt Swinton came in a little apologetically, hauling off his worn sombrero.

"You wanted me, Mr. Puryear?" he asked as he closed the door behind him.

Boyce Puryear nodded. "Yes," he said curtly. "Lock that door there, Newt, and sit down. I've got some things to talk about. That Renfrow hombre all safe?"

Swinton laughed sourly. "He ain't come to yet," he informed. "A little more English on Zeb's gun butt and he wouldn't a' been botherin' nobody no more a-tall."

Puryear grunted. He was a big man, getting along toward fifty, with piercing black eyes and stern thick lips that had a bluish tinge. Iron gray hair grew thickly on his large head but it had no softening effect on his hard face, almost vulpine with its hawk nose and thick, shaggy eyebrows. Not the face of a man on whom any woman could ever look tenderly, but one on which men would look—and fear.

The sheriff of Comal drew up his chair and sat down, and the four men at once became engaged in close and most private conversation. Besides Puryear and Swinton, there was Putt Ratliff, burly and rat-eyed foreman of the K Breeching K spread who had taken matters into his own hands out on the road, and Luke Brundett, well-dressed, but gangling and hawk-eyed president of the Stockmen's Bank of Hondo. But dominating the whole venomous-eyed, brutal-minded quartet was Boyce Puryear himself, even when he said nothing—Puryear, owner of the K Breeching K, and virtual czar of Comal Basin, the man who would make his rule absolute.

Putt Ratliff, cold as a sidewinder, took up his talk where he had left it off on the sheriff's entrance.

"As I was sayin'," he remarked, "now that Kuykendall and Lacey have left town—"

120

The Sheriff nodded. "Yeah, about an hour ago—headed for the Rafter M ranch, they said . . . They're buryin' Lynn Merrill this evenin'."

"Uh-huh." Ratliff nodded. "An' it's my say-so that the quicker that hombre Renfrow snakes to hell through a riata, the better, an' I reckon you all know why . . . Zach's plumb shore it was that hombre he saw when he was on the shelf above the spring. Which same means he must a' been somewheres around when Merrill got his, an' if this Renfrow is give a trial like Kuykendall and Lacey is insistin', an' he gets to shootin' off his mouth, why no tellin'—"

Sheriff Newt put in hastily, then: "He's plumb right, boss. Them two Blanco Creek ranchers didn't fall so heavy for our play this mornin', and I don't think the Merrill gal did either, so—"

Puryear frowned heavily and growled: "Leave her out of this. I'll attend to her."

Putt Ratliff remarked, as though idly, with a slight suggestion of a laugh: "I was bearin' something about how this Renfrow hombre might a' headed this way to see her, but I reckon there warn't nothin' to that talk." He went on, without apparently noticing the glower on the face of his grizzled boss, though his words had been carefully chosen for their effect: "What I say is, we've got this feller in our hands now, we got things headed all our own way—and we might as well do it up brown."

"Yes," nodded Luke Brundett, pursing his thin lips, tapping his fingers together as was his custom in a board meeting, and speaking as primly. "Let's see. Today is Friday. Tuesday morning, Puryear, unless a miracle happens to prevent it, you'll have possession of Twin Springs." He cleared his throat, added hesitantly: "But—ah—I am inclined to agree with Ratliff. There is one man who might make things a bit—ah—awkward . . . What about this Renfrow? If it should prove true he did not come to Hondo from the *east,* as he has been saying, that he should have a story to be investigated, why—" He glanced at Puryear who was frowning heavily, his chin sunk on his chest. "Certain plans have been made for his—ah—disposition, Puryear?"

The big man's head came up with a jerk, and his frown grew deeper.

"Listen!" the boss of Comal snapped abruptly, leaning forward, his tone barely above a harsh whisper. "I've been planning for all that. Your talk about lynching won't do. There would be too many questions. I've got a better plan." His voice lowered still more. "Renfrow," he said decisively, "will be shot and killed trying to escape from jail—downed by the high sheriff of Comal, acting in the discharge of his duty." Quickly he unfolded for the benefit of his confreres the plan he had concocted as a fitting finish for the permanent removal of the troublesome prisoner. He leaned back with a satisfied smile on his heavy features as he finished, nodding:

"And it'll look plumb right and proper, too, far as we're concerned." He laughed nastily. "Looks from where I see it that it might be a long time before this hombre that calls himself Ace Renfrow and has maybe come a-courtin' from the Panhandle can do it—if they do any courtin' where he's headed for."

There were looks of satisfaction on the faces of his listeners, and relief that the matter could so easily be attended to. More than one man in and around Hondo had no desire whatever for their prisoner to get a chance to tell his story publicly, no matter what it was.

"Damned good plan," Ratliff agreed, and his sentiment was echoed by the others. "You're the one to think it out, I've always said. We ain't never made no mistake leavin' all the headwork to you, boss."

Boyce Puryear smiled complacently as he arose. Why should he not smile? Things were moving his way. They always did. It was his intention they always should. He beckoned to the others as he walked to the door, unlocked it.

"Come and have a drink," he invited. "Looks like some kind of a toast is in order for—some-body—huh?"

CHAPTER X
CHOLLA MAKES A BREAK

THE afterglow of sunset painted the sky above the Ramireñas, and the wide sweep of mesquite and sage was darkening into shadow. Only the last dancing gold and crimson and purple touches lingered, reluctant to go, on the highest crags and hilltops. Clouded blue twilight smudged the Hondo jail and its cell block, and Ace Sutton, seated on the edge of his bunk, was just a vague shadow among many shadows. He sat motion-less, hands between his knees, cold quirly in his mouth, eyes steely gray and grim, cutting through the gathering gloom. But his nerves were as cold as his dead cigarette; every muscle was tensed and taut as he considered his position in the cold-deck town.

Vague and without its disturbing his painful reverie he heard some one enter the sheriff's office and light a lamp. In a moment the peace officer came into the cell corridor and put match to the two bracketed lamps on the wall opposite the four cells. There was a sneer on Newt Swinton's lips beneath his drooping, stained mustaches as he stopped for a moment to squint in at his lone prisoner. But he did not deign to speak a word to Cholla.

He went back to his office, and the prisoner could hear him clomping about in there. He could hear a mumble of words as some one came to the outer door, spoke a moment or two, and almost immediately retired. Then presently the sheriff returned to the cells, carrying with him a plate of food and a tin cup of coffee.

Placing these on the floor, while he unlocked the steel grating, he entered Cholla's cell with drawn gun in one hand and plate in the other, gruffly ordering the cowboy to sit where he was, and to make no move. Easing the food to the floor, with his gun not wavering from where he had it trained on his prisoner, Swinton backed out and closed the door behind him. He had clomped out of sight, spurs jingling against the stone floor before the Cholla Kid picked up the plate and cup and sat down again with them on his knees.

Frijole beans, soggy baking powder biscuits, cold potatoes. Lukewarm coffee, doused with blue-john milk. Hungry as he was, Cholla eyed the repast distastefully, a sudden homesick feeling tugging at his heart as he could almost smell the tang of his own campfire and the sizzling of bacon in his frying pan.

So intent had he been on his own thoughts, in which a blue-eyed girl and the wrongs done her were strangely mixed up, that he had completely failed to note the absence of the click of the cell door lock as it had swung shut behind the sheriff, nor did he realize that the grill was not self-locking. It had not occurred to him to investigate, either. Men such as these in Hondo would not be apt to be the careless kind in making preparations to hold their prisoners.

More or less mechanically he attacked the soggy mess, however, and as he ate, his mind was reviewing all that had occurred to land him in his present predicament. The Cholla Kid had been in tight places before, had rather gloried in his reputation as a hell-raiser, always fighting Mexes, always cleaning out bars, always starting a riot in some town when he raced into it with his pay in his pockets and too much exuberance in his system. But never had he done anything that could really pin on him the tag of outlaw—not until that last time in that little town the other side of Mobeetie. He was not so sure now he should have got out of town the way he did and not stayed to face the music.

But it had not looked so good. He knew he would have a better chance if he stayed away a while and then went back when some of the hotheads had cooled down. He had raised a little too much devilment, and those men had not been in a mood for explanations. Pretty much of a cold deck town, too, overrun with Mexes, but not like this Hondo. Here, it looked as if he would not have any chance at all, and in spite of anything he might have done, he had always thought that if he ever did have to die suddenly, it would be with both his smoke poles in his hands.

That affair back in the Panhandle—the Cholla Kid had no special twinges of conscience about it. Any man with a mite of spirit would have done what he had. Catching a bunch of thieving Mexes cheating at stud poker and bringing them to turn wasn't anything to make a man light a shuck away from home, but the way it had happened—

The scene was plain before Cholla's eyes. The two sharps he had found working in cahoots against him—coming in on him good and proper until he got from his seat saying, politely: "All bets are off, gents. I'll take my money back."

The gambler's sneer—"You're talkin' like a cantina gal, gringo! You tryin' to say this game's crooked?"

"You got it the first time—it is, because I caught that barkeep signallin'—Get up, I'm goin' to work you two over."

The rasp from one of the crooks, before all hell broke loose in the bar-room, as a gun came like lightning from a Mex's holster: "Claw the air, gringo—we got the drop on you."

Cholla smiled grimly, remembering how he had "clawed", but there had been shooting irons in both his hands when he did it. All he had seen for a moment was the grin wiped off the gambling rattler's mouth as a slug hit it. The other gun had caught the other crook's arm while he was drawing on Cholla and the moment before the Cholla Kid had dodged the bottle of red-eye hurled at him by the barkeeper. That worthy, Cholla had an idea, was running yet if the howl he let out of him leaping to the door as a Cholla Kid bullet smashed the mirror behind him, was anything to go by.

Much of it was a blur, after that, with a memory of the Mex proprietor coming a-shagging in the door with a sawed-off shot-gun in his hand, and yelling for the sheriff. A hombre half-Mex, half white, that sheriff was, and he was trailing right behind.

Cholla had wasted no time and he had a vision of Mexicans sprawling as he shot, and others stampeding out of the place faster than anything he ever remembered outside of a herd of cattle caught in a storm.

Somebody had caught Cholla with a slug that tore off his sombrero and a chunk of scalp with it, and then the sheriff was on him, howling for him to surrender. Cholla had "surrendered" to that particular sheriff by handing him an uppercut that ought to have dislocated his head from his spine. It laid him out for a balmy sleep before he could use his gun—about the deadest-looking carcass Cholla had ever seen outside of Soda Mesa.

Not dead, of course—men didn't go to Boot

129

Hill from wallops on the jaw. But because the fellow *was* the sheriff, and it was about then that there had come from down the street a yipping and a shouting and the clatter and thunder of horses' hoofs, a still small voice of warning had informed the Cholla Kid that he had better be on his way pronto, and do his explaining afterwards. There had not been enough white men around, and he knew he hadn't a Chinaman's chance if caught. That mob of *vaqueros* would act, and do *their* explaining afterwards.

So the Cholla Kid had shot his way out of town, and thus far had not gone back. Handbills he had run across had apprised him that he was wanted back there, and another handbill or two had been stuck up from other towns that wanted the Cholla Kid for helling, but there were no charges of murder against him—which proved to him that he had left no "corpus delictis" behind.

Once started, he had kept going. It was as good a time as any to see the country. It was a reasonable idea, he considered, to give some of them back in New Mex plenty of chance to cool down.

That was how it stood when he had reached the Ramireñas. Now here he was! This town of Hondo was a different proposition. It would take plenty to get him out of this sweet mess. From where the Cholla Kid sat in the Hondo jail it didn't look so good.

As he mused he was making an attempt to get rid of the frijole beans and try not to taste them too much. Subconsciously he was aware that men were coming and going outside. He heard a number of them enter the sheriff's office, but could not hear their conversation, carried on in husky, subdued tones. Moreover, the cell block door was closed.

Just as one of the visitors was evidently preparing to leave, the sheriff came to the cell block door, opened it, apparently with the intention of entering. Something must have changed his mind, for he shut it again. But in that short interval while the door was opened its crack, Cholla distinctly heard a man's voice rumble:

"Good huntin', Newt. Be seein' you *pronto*." And a laugh. "The big boss can't never say you ain't done nothin' for him, huh?"

Eyes narrowed speculatively, Cholla set aside his empty plate and cup and curled a smoke. Presently he got to his feet and walked over toward the small square of window above his bunk. It was too high above his head for him to see out, but stepping up on the bunk, he balanced himself, gazing thoughtfully through its grill. In the blue of twilight he could see that there were things afoot in that town. Instinct told him he was a central figure in what was expected to occur.

Probably but few men in the town knew what was actually planned—Cholla could only make a grim guess himself—but there was an air of tenseness, expectancy, in every man who passed the jail. He saw numbers of men passing, singly and in groups, from his narrow vantage point, half screened as it was with greasewood trees and tangled mesquite that no one had troubled to clear away.

Closer to the plaza, groups of townsmen and rough cowboys were gathered on the board sidewalks, and in the dusty street, talking in low tones. A sinister something, like a gray pall, hung over the whole town. Men apparently were waiting for threatened violent death in some form—brutal-visaged men from town and nearby ranches, gunmen, killers in the eyes of the Cholla Kid who knew the breed; men who swaggered and laughed loud.

The man inside the jail window tightened his lips into a mirthless grin, as a single word rasped from his throat:

"Coyotes!"

When it grew too dark for him to longer see into the street, imagining the men in bars discussing him as the man who had dry-gulched Lynn Merrill, Cholla turned from the grill and began a cat-footed prowl around the cell.

Halting his prowl by the cell block door, he leaned against it carelessly—and the grill portal swung outward! Nearly keeled off balance by the unexpected movement, Cholla recovered his equilibrium by a quick forward leap and stood crouched in the corridor, slitted eyes fixed upon the closed door of the sheriff's office. And his sixth sense was clicking to him a message more rapidly than any before had ever been tapped into his brain. It dawned on him what it meant—that closed door! And what Putt Ratliff's words—he was sure now that it had been Ratliff's voice he had heard!—had meant!

Cholla's lip curled back over his teeth in a soundless snarl. Good hunting, eh? Yeah. Meaning that that rattlesnake Ratliff wished the sheriff lots of luck in murdering his lone prisoner. Probably that was just why the Cholla Kid *was* a lone prisoner. He had not thought about it before, but it was strange that a town like Hondo should have its jail empty so conveniently. There must have been others there. Removed, of course, before the Cholla Kid was chucked in. And now Putt Ratliff, foreman for Boyce Puryear, the czar of Comal Basin, was hoping its sheriff would find his latest job an easy one!

Slipping back inside the grilled cell door, closing it after him, Cholla found his way back to his cot through the semi-darkness. For perhaps twenty minutes, he sat on the edge of the bunk, waiting, pondering his chances. Or if he had a chance at all. His enemies had tipped their hand all right, and the only thing in Cholla's favor so far as he could see now was that they had no

133

idea of it. They certainly wanted to get rid of one Cholla Sutton, and meant to see to it there should be no chance of his giving them the slip, legally or otherwise. Not content with framing him for murder, they now intended to place him in their Boot Hill, plumb out of the way.

Frame-up! That was what that silent pall holding the town in its grip had been whispering, had been saying to Cholla by the very tenseness of body of every man who stalked the dusty streets of Hondo. But there had been more. All the men in town were not Puryear's men. They, too, must be there for a purpose. Puryear and his cohorts must have realized that, must know they were not safe with a frame-up. Tension was in the very air, as if six-guns were ready to spew and bellow with sudden death if this affair of the man Renfrow should be shown to be a frame-up and thus precipitate the long-smouldering show-down between Puryear's crowd and all the honest cattlemen left in the Comal Basin. Little as he knew of the situation thereabouts, Cholla knew that such a showdown could only end in wholesale killings.

No, they would not risk that. There was only one obvious course for them to take, and they were taking it. They meant to get rid of the man who called himself Renfrow in some other way— and quickly—before he got a chance to shoot off his mouth.

Every nerve in Cholla's body felt like ice as full realization came to him. Well, it was up to him now. Some way he would have to figure it out. But he must make the breaks, now, not wait for his enemies to act.

A soft sound outside the grill work of the little window did not at first come to his abstracted attention. It came again, and he noticed it, something like the swishing of the greasewood trees against the glassless opening, as if the trees were whispering. Suddenly, when it came a third time, he jerked up his head. It *was* whispering. Somewhere outside there was somebody—a human being—trying to make him hear, without being heard by others.

Soundlessly he leaped to his feet, cat-footed it to the head of his cot and stepped up. The whisper became words, as his eyes saw a bulking shadow outside. It took on the form of a horseman near the grill, hidden in the shadows of the trees.

"Hey, Renfrow!" The whisper came sibilantly. "Where are you?"

Cholla saw then that the horseman was Kip Helm, foreman of the Rafter M. Sanna Merrill's foreman! She had not forgotten then, even on this terrible day with her grief and with burying her father! And those ranchers, her friends, had meant what they had said when they told him they were with him—every way. They would need to be to help him now. There was no longer a chance of fair fighting.

Cholla's cautious whisper went through the grill.

"Right here—Quiet! The sheriff's inside."

He saw Kip's nod, and then the horse was moved silently close against the building, beside the window. Cholla pressed his face against the grating, hope surging exultant in his heart. Kip was whispering good news. He and a bunch of the boys from neighboring ranches had slipped into town, and were ready to mask up with bandannas, knock Swinton for a loop, and make a jail delivery just as soon as Hondo had quieted down for the night. Jeff Kuykendall, Bart Lacey, and a few others of the honest cowmen savvied all about the plan, were in it to the hilt, and their cowboys were raring to go.

Then Cholla sprung his own whispered surprise. In a few terse words he acquainted Kip with the plot against him, finishing by announcing with some brim-stone-worded embroidery that he could get out of that *juzgado* damned pronto if Kip would lend him a gun. The Rafter M foreman cursed fervently, in a low monotone, as he shoved his heavy .45 through the window grating.

"Buzzards! Rattlers! Poison vinagarroons!" he grated, but before he moved his horse back he repeated grimly: "We'll be waitin' for you . . . Good huntin', cowboy!"

Straightening as he stepped off the bunk, Cholla dropped his quirly stub, crushing it with his heel. Unconsciously he rubbed his palms along the sides of his legs, for the feel of the guns that were not there. Lifting the weapon the foreman had shoved to him, he spun the cylinder, and thumbing a cartridge under the hammer, snapped it shut. He was ready now!

Bending, he picked up the china plate and tin cup from where he had set them, and smashed them both against the cell block floor with terrific force, sidling against the wall as he did so, gun held low, but ready.

A chair scraped on the floor in the front office. Footsteps clumped toward the corridor door. It opened raspily. The sheriff stepped into the dusky passage, hand on gun, and saw the vague smudge of his prisoner near the open door of his cell. The peace officer stiffened.

"Why, dang my eyes!" he bawled, in well-feigned surprise and anger. Cholla knew on the instant that he was not without an unseen audience, somebody who could swear to the truth of what the high sheriff of Comal meant later to say. "Whatcha doin' out here, you murderin' polecat? One o' these here smart hombres, I betcha, that boasts airy jail won't hold 'em! Tryin' to git gay with *me,* are you?" His hand swung up as he bellowed: "Well, see if you can stop this, hombre!"

Prepared for it, Cholla ducked. The sheriff's bullet sang past him and struck the wall of the corridor with a thud. But Cholla, firing the instant before, had put a stop to any second bullet, or any further words from Sheriff Newt Swinton forever. The heavy slug was put flush through the eyes of Boyce Puryear's purchased official murderer.

A lamp burned in the sheriff's office as Cholla stepped over the lanky body and slipped into the front of the jail. The front door was open and two scrawny old men were just disappearing through it, high-tailing it down the street. Cholla recognized one of them—the old clerk of the Medina House. His quick eye caught sight of the bottle and glasses on the desk. Witnesses, of course. The sheriff had thought he had no need of gunmen, and he had been entertaining the old clerk and an ancient crony. Their word could not possibly be doubted. There was a grim smile on Cholla's lips as he darted through the door. Fate had given him one good break in having all the gun fighters in Hondo safely in the bar rooms where their own alibis could be proven.

Darting into the shadows, Cholla cautiously made his way from the jail. Circling the west block of the square, following Kip Helm's instructions, he soon found himself among a group of shadowy horsemen, who awaited him behind the Ranny's Roost saloon. Hard-faced, thin-lipped riders who had not failed him in his hour of need; men whose mounts bore the brands of L Open A, Bar Lazy 3 Slash, Clover Leaf, Rafter M. Men who had not hesitated to tangle with the law for him, nor to buck Boyce Puryear and all his gun-slinging rowdies in their own stronghold.

As they quietly sifted out of town toward the upper basin, Cholla answered questions and gave a full report of all that had happened in the jail. As dramatic as had been the real occurrence, Cholla, in the terse-worded way of men of the range, did not take long to tell his story, nor to answer all of their questions.

For a while the cavalcade rode on in silence. Where, Cholla paid no heed at first. Finally it occurred to him to ask Kip where they were headed.

"These hombres with us are goin' to a little powwow over to Twin Springs, Kip drawled. "A few little matters maybe needin' attention right soon over that-away. Me'n you are headed for the Rafter M to make some *habla* with the boss. She seemed right shore you'd be along." He grinned a little drily, before he added: "And after that—Well, I reckon you'll have to light a shuck to the tall and uncut for a spell—lay low. Puryear's bunch o' hellions would stretch your neck quicker'n scat if they was to catch you now. You done kilt their high sheriff, you know, Renfrow—" he grinned. "Umm, I meant Cholla."

Yeah, Cholla reflected, not too highly pleased at the thought, he knew. His lips were mumbling as he bent over the neck of his borrowed horse, as if the mount had been Jerky:

"Yeah, I've got a shore 'nuff killin' on my hands now."

CHAPTER XI
SANNA'S DEFY

AS early as sunup the following morning the plaza of Hondo swarmed with armed men. The killing of Sheriff Newt Swinton at the Hondo jail the night before was on every man's tongue. Men waited for more death in the rough town ringed by mountains and range.

Before the stores, in the plaza itself, and on the board sidewalks they gathered in knots and whispered the killing and escape story grimly, amidst threats of ominous reprisals. Tense-faced, they talked in low tones, while gun-butts bristled in the early morning light. Everywhere a humming state of excitement prevailed.

Boyce Puryear who had hurriedly come in to town the night before from the K Breeching K when a galloping horseman had brought him the news, again sat in his private room at the Legal Tender. Narrow-eyed and hard-faced, savagely chewing an unlighted cigar, he went over the unexpected and far from agreeable situation with his most trusted men.

Putt Ratliff was present, as before, but the bank president was not this time called into a

141

consultation that would have more to do with war than with cunning planning. In his stead, and in place of the dead sheriff, Creed Calkins and Blease Lanfear now sat in chairs opposite the boss of Comal. Calkins was ostensibly the owner of the Legal Tender, though it was generally known that Puryear was the real owner of the place as well as of the Medina House across the street, and most of the other places of importance in Hondo. Blease Lanfear was Calkin's *segundo*, the man who served behind the bar when the supposed owner was busy on other work for Puryear—Lanfear, the man the Cholla Kid had spotted the minute he entered the Legal Tender as too sleek, a bit, for his job.

Puryear was in a vile temper at the escape of the prisoner. He was worried, too, which he realized it would not do to have known. He took it out in blasphemously blaming everybody in the town for the affair, as futilely as he blamed the dead sheriff.

"He's got to be caught!" he repeated viciously, the burden of his complaint from the first. "Here everything was going fine, we were all sitting pretty, and that so-and-such has to go and turn a joker in the game! Can't for the life of me see how Newt ever let him come Injun on him good and proper like that. We'd ought to have found out more about that Renfrow hombre while we had the chance. Now we don't know anything—even if he's packin' a star—"

"But we do know he done for the high sheriff, Boss," Calkins put in with an attempt at soothing. "And that's more'n a good and plenty for us to hit out after him hell bent."

"Yeah, he's got to be caught!" Puryear was roaring again. "And maybe that won't be so easy as it looks! He must have had some outside help—he's likely still got it! How else could he have got that gun?" His jaws clamped down, and he gritted out: "I've got a pretty fair idea who helped him, too, damn 'em!"

"Me'n you both, boss," said Putt Ratliff, sourly. "There's a gang o' hombres up valley that ain't bein' fooled much by our plans, and they'd shore like to put a spoke in our wheels, even if they had to get some outside star-packer to help 'em. You know who I mean—Helm, Kuykendall, Groce o' the Clover Leaf, Standifer and Cozine, L Open A—that Blanco Creek crowd. But I don't believe Renfrow's very far away . . . Like as not that gang don't want him far away."

The yellow-bearded Calkins grunted.

"Maybe so," he growled. "But he's some-where's where we don't seem to be able to lay our hands on him. We didn't find hair nor hide of him last night when we lit out for him right after he made his get-away from the jail. Searched all around the Rafter M special, seein' some o' them were sayin' he had known Lynn Merrill. We

143

went there after we got through with all the other ranches that are so dead set against you, Boss. Looked everywhere for sign. Nothin' doin'. I got an idea he's lit a shuck for the hills, figgerin' we got both necks o' the Basin corked up. Don't know just how he got out o' town—nobody saw anybody leavin' after Newt was done for, except seein' a few cowboys from the Slash and the Clover Leaf and a few that had been hittin' it up in honkytonk town. But he shore managed to get a hoss somewheres, for his pinto's still in the stable, along with his war-sack and saddle."

"And see that it stays there!" grated Puryear. He got to his feet, towering above his henchmen as he stalked about, head lowered in deep thought. Finally he straightened and shot out some orders. "Place a man on guard at that stable, Calkins— Sid Grumbles is not much more than a fool. And you, Putt, you act as temporary sheriff—say it's my orders—appoint any deputies you want. Lanfear can leave the bar here and look after the ranch end of things. The thousand dollars reward I've offered for Renfrow's apprehension ought to put a cocklebur under a lot of saddle blankets hereabouts. But if no news comes in by dinner time, I aim to increase it by a couple of thousand. I'm willing to go to any length to get the murderer of this county's sheriff, my old friend—" he did not see the sly grin which the sleek Lanfear hid behind his hand at the pompous announcement,

144

but went right on, never stopping in his pacing the room: "See that any doubtful spreads are kept under observation. You know well enough which they are. I aim to stay right here in town, at the hotel, until things break one way or another."

He glanced up at the men who had waited silently for him to finish. With a wave of his hand he dismissed them.

"That's all—right now. Just see your foot don't slip—like Newt Swinton's did."

"Okay, Boss," said Ratliff, as he got up and sauntered toward the door. "We'll trail that hombre down for you—or *else*."

The sun was getting higher, sending its rays down brassily when Sanna Merrill, accompanied by the bleak-faced Kip Helm, drew rein on her white-faced mare in front of the Stockmen's Bank on the plaza. Luke Brundett, president, saw her through the window before she swung from her horse lightly and headed for the bank. Entering it, she made directly for his sanctum, as he had imagined she would. There was a thin smile on his wrinkled lips and his sunken eyes were cold.

Though Brundett knew that the girl's days of grace were all but finished on one of her accounts, he had not expected her the first thing on Saturday morning, the bank's half day, and only hours after her father had been buried. If he expected her at all. He was certain in his own mind that Sanna Merrill's visit could mean but one thing—to find out if the bank was willing to renew the combined chattel mortgage and lien on the Twin Springs section, due three days later, on Tuesday morning. His head was bent over his desk and he appeared not to have seen her through the glass partition as she neared.

"Come in," he growled, at her rap on his door.

Sanna entered, nodding shortly. She wasted scant time in small talk. After listening to the president's hypocritical condolences in regard to her father's death, she got right down to cases.

"You know why I am here, Mr. Brundett," she said crisply. "You may have been expecting a call from me now that my father is gone. I want to see about the lien and mortgage due next week on Twin Springs."

"Ah, yes," said Brundett, in his best official manner, pressing his fingertips together and pursing his thin lips. "Er—it's difficult for me to speak on a business matter to a young lady so lately bereaved, but what—ah—do you propose to do about it, Miss Sanna?"

"Perhaps that's for you to say, Mr. Brundett," said Sanna calmly. "I'd like a sixty-day extension. Until after the round-up, anyhow. I think then that I can manage to pay off."

Brundett cleared his throat. "That will be impossible, I fear," he said coldly. "I must follow the will of the bank directors. Mr. Puryear has himself taken this whole thing over from the bank, transferred it to his personal account. He owns the controlling interest in the bank, as you must know, and it happens that he wants your Twin Springs range, Miss Merrill." He shrugged and spread out thin, wizened hands that belied his metaphorical words. "My hands are tied."

Sanna's lips whitened and her hands gripped together hard.

"You mean that if the twenty-seven hundred dollars is not paid at once, that is, by next Tuesday morning, in spite of there being no time to settle my father's affairs, to see how matters stand, that you intend to foreclose on the dot?"

"Such are Mr. Puryear's directions," said Brundett, icily. Then he glanced at the girl, as if considering. "If I might give you a bit of fatherly advice, Miss Sanna? Could I suggest that you might personally speak to Mr. Puryear, as I might say without betraying any—ah—confidences— could you say to him that you have reconsidered some of your own most personal feelings about him, it might be—"

Sanna jumped to her feet, her eyes blazing.

"You're trying to say that I might keep Twin Springs if I'm willing to take Boyce Puryear along with it?" she spat out. "Then you can hear what I've told him—no, *thank* you!" Then some of the spirit in her died as she realized what keeping that property had meant to her father, how she had silently promised him to fight the fight. "You—you don't mean to say there's no other way. That you *will* foreclose?"

Brundett shrugged his thin, well-clad shoulders.

"Mr. Puryear's instructions were quite clear on the point of foreclosure," he said drily. "What I have said was in a friendly spirit, though you may not choose to think it so. Mr. Puryear is quite ignorant that I may have taken it on myself to point out to you an alternative; may not thank me for it."

"Doubtless," she retorted bitterly. "But Mr. Boyce Puryear will be compelled to acquire Twin Springs and the Rafter M without marrying it. Mr. Brundett." Her eyes felt bright with angry tears, but she held them back, spoke coolly. "Well, I see I am wasting my time in asking for an extension. But there's one other very important thing, Mr. Brundett. About that money recovered in the Medina House. Newt Swinton, who so triumphantly told of its recovery in his desire to declare the man Renfrow my father's murderer, was quite right—in one thing. That money *was* my father's. He went to San Saba after it. It was—and *is*—his. He was robbed, and I have plenty of witnesses who heard Newt Swinton boast that the money had been recovered. I happen to know the exact amount my father went after, and he was robbed of it—five thousand, three hundred dollars. It was recovered, so Swinton said, (and

I happen to know that Puryear also has been boasting about that) in a mattress in a room at the Medina House. I presume that is mine now, along with whatever else my father left, and so it can be turned over to me at once. I can pay the lien and mortgage with it, after all."

Brundett smiled sourly, scratching his chin. His eyes were hooded.

"Er—" he said hesitantly, searching about in his mind for an answer to that straight speech, damning Boyce Puryear for not having thought of it "there is—ah—a question about that, Miss Merrill. The matter has already been taken up and the district attorney, Bratcher, as well as Lawyer Ackrood, have handed down opinions in regard to it. Both agree that the matter must be settled according to law, which will take some time, naturally. The money, which is—ah—you might say, in the nature of state's evidence, cannot be handed over to you until that man Renfrow who stole it when he murdered your father—which is the general opinion, and which his murdering Newt Swinton bears out—is apprehended and tried for his crime. Until then it must remain in trust."

Sanna Merrill sprang to her feet again, her lithe body, clad in its corduroy riding suit, trembling, her blue eyes flaming with wrath.

"You bunch of crooked side-winders!" she burst out, her hands gripping at her sides in her desire to spring at this fish-eyed man and rend him. "All of you! Puryear—Bratcher—Ackrood—*you*—all working hand-in-glove! The old game of freeze-out for me, just as you were trying to work it on Dad who would have been too smart for you! Just as you've frozen out lots of smaller ranchers than we all through Comal Basin!" She threw back her head and her laugh was not a pleasant one for the man to hear. "Well, I'm a gambler, Luke Brundett! My father taught me to be one, to play the game according to the rules—and not to be afraid!" In her heart she felt that her father must be standing beside her when she said that, urging her to remember his teachings, even as she recalled his words. "I still have a few days to raise that money, and I'll raise it! Hold onto Dad's money that *somebody* took off his dead body all you please, but you'll never get Twin Springs!"

As she turned passionately away, he said suavely:

"I suppose you've heard, Miss Merrill, that the murderer of your father, whose capture you witnessed, one Ace Renfrow, as he called himself, escaped from jail last night after killing the sheriff?"

"Yes," she repeated sardonically. "I *have* heard. With armed possemen riding all over my ranch in the dark, shouting and cursing, apparently with the idea that I might give harbor to my father's 'murderer' a few hours after I had buried Dad on the hill back of the hacienda, I couldn't help but hear. It was astonishing news. Good morning."

"Also," Brundett said, as he got up and followed her to the door, an unmistakable inflection in his tone, "there is a reward for Renfrow's capture, dead or alive—offered by our most public-spirited citizen, Boyce Puryear." He had to lay his hand on her arm to detain her a second while he finished, as Sanna flung open the door. And he said: "That amount would go far toward relieving the indebtedness due on your Twin Springs section—"

Sanna Merrill looked him straight in the eye, one hand on the door-knob.

"A lot of things can happen in three days, Señor Brundett," she said coolly. "A lot of things have been known to happen in one night. Once, one night when the game was going against me, I drew to an inside straight—*and filled it!*"

CHAPTER XII
CHOLLA MARCHES ON THE ENEMY

WITH the hiding place that had been selected for the Cholla Kid, it was not strange that Boyce Puryear's hastily assembled posse had not found him after his dramatic escape from the Hondo jail. All the time men had been galloping and cursing over the ranches, searching bunk houses and outbuildings, haylofts and all the surrounding territory, Cholla was sleeping peacefully, getting some much-needed repose—rest of which he would later be in still greater need. He was in the last spot that could have been suspected.

While Sanna Merrill sat quietly in the lighted living room of her ranch house, pretending to read a book she could not see with eyes bright with unshed tears, but where the rough possemen who might look through windows could see her, Cholla Sutton was asleep under her roof. Well guarded, too, though there were no men with guns about him.

The riotous sounds outside when men searched the Rafter M ranch did not disturb him as he snoozed quietly in old Maria's cubby hole room back of the kitchen. The old Mexican woman herself sat in the middle of the floor, nodding, as she kept guard.

It was nearing daylight when the last signs of the men searching for Cholla were gone. Kip Helm, finally assured they were all gone, slipped in to tell Sanna the coast was clear. Then it was that in old Maria's room, Sanna and Cholla and Kip had their delayed *"habla,"* with much to be told and many plans to be made. It was there, too, that Cholla learned, when other matters had been discussed, that his suspicion that the boss of the Comal Basin wanted to make Sanna his wife was confirmed. It was a ticklish subject, one on which he hated to ask questions, but Cholla had to know.

"As if I would think of such a thing!" Sanna said, her head lifted defiantly. "Even if I didn't know how long he made life unbearable for Dad, trying to get everything we owned! And even if I wasn't positive now that Boyce Puryear is responsible for my father's murder!"

Cholla had to look away to hold down the rage inside him as he saw her trembling lips and the wistful expression in her eyes. Brave as she was, the girl had stood about all that she could. He only nodded, and it was Kip Helm who spoke:

"Just you keep your head up, Sanna," he encouraged. "We ain't licked yet, and your dad would like to know we're goin' on . . . You ain't goin' to lose your prop'ty—someway the boys

154

are goin' to see to that if they have to plumb clean out that nest of rattlers over at the K Breechin' K."

Sanna's eyes blazed furiously as she burst out:

"Oh, they ought to be—every one of them! They're all murderers, the whole lot of them!—everybody knows that, but they've always got away with still another kind of murder with Puryear behind them. I don't see what any of the honest ranchers really can do, Kip, when you come down to it. . . . Puryear's gang is strong, with more gun fighters, hired and otherwise, than the rest of us could get together, and it would only mean murder to attack them—more murder, and God knows we've had enough of that!"

The Cholla Kid made no answer to her outburst, calmly lighting another brownie while he sat deep in thought. If Sanna had known what was in his mind, she would not have herself sat so quietly planning for the safety of the Cholla Kid until there should come the time when he could come out of hiding and ally himself with her handful of rancher friends against the common enemy.

In that dimly lighted room she could not well see his face, his eyes, nor could she have read what was behind them if she had. His face was as bleak as glacier ice under an arctic moon while he listened to fuller details of all the killings and

155

depredations that could be laid to the owner of the K Breeching K and his murder band.

The Cholla Kid was telling himself: This blue-eyed girl whom Boyce Puryear had doubly tortured because he could not have her for his own, who in his greed wanted to grab the whole Basin, wanted Puryear's "nest of rattlers" cleaned out. She and her friends were even then laying their plans toward that end. In the nature of things they could not take the chances the Cholla Kid could. He was as free as the air of the ranges. It did not so much matter what happened to him, and he could do no more than die trying.

She wanted them cleaned out? All right— she would be surprised probably, at the speed with which some of them would claw the dust of their stolen range land. They were after the scalp of the Cholla Kid, too, had framed him for the nastiest murder known to the West—dry-gulching and robbery. Now it was a question of who should and would get in the quickest and surest shots.

Cholla gave Sanna Merrill no intimation of what was his purpose, though, when he left her, after getting outside of the substantial breakfast which old Maria prepared. Not even Kip had any faintest idea of the reckless mission Cholla planned when he had a few more whispered words with the foreman outside. Kip was leading him to a tough little sorrel pony full of stamina that Kip believed would take the Panhandle cowboy speedily to the Ramireña hills.

"You just keep ridin', cowboy," Kip advised. "Make for the hills—it's not safe tryin' to get out of the Basin now. You'll meet up later with Jeff where Miss Sanna said, and you can have a powwow with him about what you can do in this here to help. I wouldn't like the new young boss to know it, but if you're askin' me, it's beginnin' to look mighty like range war's liable to bust out any minute does this Puryear take away the Merrills' Twin Springs. Then God help us!"

Cholla said nothing to that, only nodded. No one knew better than he what hell it would mean if range war should come, especially in the face of Puryear's long preparations for it. The outlaw gunmen he had imported were spoiling for just that thing. Somehow or other it would have to be stopped before it started, and he had more than a vague idea that it was the Cholla Kid who was elected, unbeknown to any of them—to Sanna Merrill, in particular—to do the starting.

With grub to last him for days, he rode silently away from the Rafter M, headed as Kip had indicated, for the Ramireñas. It was still dark, the velvet-black dark that always comes before the first flush of dawn. He could be far on his way before the first streaks of light. And in his brain, as he went along at a jog trot, his pony's hoofs

157

making only soft, padded sounds, there was being repeated over and over the words of a blue-eyed girl, whose firm hand-grip in parting still tingled his hand:

"I believe in and trust you, Ace Sutton . . . And I'm sure that someway you're going to help us find who killed my father—That terrible crowd has got to be brought to justice."

There was a grim smile on the Cholla Kid's face as he rode on in the darkness. She was right. She might be surprised *how!*

Daylight came on quickly, almost as soon as Cholla had reached the foothills and headed for the woodsy tangles of the hillsides. Kip had said it was best for his purpose that he hide out there through the hours of daylight. In a hidden glen he finally dismounted, pushing his horse back in the scrub while he made himself comfortable for an expected wait, one that sped by more quickly than he had imagined while his thoughts were busy with his planning.

The morning was only half gone when he heard the slow clatter of horse's hoofs coming up the hillside. Cautiously he peered out of the tangle, then nodded, waiting. He was in the right place, though it had been found more or less by good guess work. That was Jeff Kuykendall meandering along. Jeff was taking it slowly, stopping from time to time as if he were searching for straying cattle.

There was a sober expression on the ranchman's face when he met Cholla in the rendezvous which had been arranged by Sanna Merrill. It was not until after the tall, hawkfaced stockman had given him a map of the Basin, with every landmark and ranch indicated thereon that he told the cowboy of the reward that had been posted for his apprehension.

"Looks bad," Kuykendall said, his head shaking. "But it's Puryear's way to get what he wants. He's after you shore enough now—he's plumb certain you know things he don't nowise want to have told—and he's gone the best way about gettin' you to have every range maverick in human form scoutin' for you because of the *pesos* he's offerin'. On the side of the law now, too, it would look like to outsiders who didn't know, and t'aint the first time he's pulled that public-spirited-citizen stuff. My advice to you, cowboy, is to hole up tight, and then slip out of this Basin soon as the Lord'll let you."

Cholla shook his head, and his eyes were glittering steel.

"I told you I was takin' a hand," he said firmly. "I don't see no need to welch right now—almost like admittin' there might be somethin' in me havin' to do with that dry-gulchin'—"

Kuykendall said quickly: "Ain't none of us thinkin' that . . . Wouldn't be, I guess, on our own, even if Sanna Merrill wasn't a-trustin'

159

you up to the hilt. All we're thinkin' about is an innocent man has been framed, that we can't seem to do much about it legal since—since— Well, anyhow, we don't aim to let any man swing for what somebody else done."

Cholla was glancing sharply at the ranchman. "You men that don't like this Puryear any more'n I do can use a good gun right soon, can't you?" he asked grimly.

Kuykendall's eyes were bleak, as he turned them from Cholla. He shook his head slowly.

" 'Course I ain't denyin' we may be needin' all the help we can get, and plenty pronto, but you're up against a frame-up, boy, you've killed a sheriff in his own jail, and—"

"And so I'm settin' in," said Cholla, with firm determination, as he stood up and held out his hand. "Thanks, Mr. Kuykendall, for this map and all, and I'll maybe be seein' you *muy pronto*." He hesitated a fractional second. "It might be I'd be lendin' you all a hand, and sort o' evenin' up things for myself, as you might say, sooner than you expect." He laughed shortly. "Hell, I didn't know my carcass was worth all o' that! A whole thousand *pesos*."

The gaunt stockman shook his head. "That's maybe only the beginnin', my boy," he informed. "You don't know Puryear like we do. He's plumb likely to raise that ante by the day or the hour, if he don't get sign of you, till every hellion in

160

the Basin'll be ridin' every inch o' this place hell bent till they get you."

"Thanks," said Cholla, again. "But I reckon I'm takin' that chance." He grinned a little. "Good huntin' to 'em, Mr. Kuykendall."

In spite of Jeff Kuykendall's advice to him to stay where he was during daylight and then work his way farther back into the hills, the Cholla Kid did not remain in his retreat much longer than it took for the stockman to make his way meanderingly out of sight. He felt confident that he could deal with any stray men he might come upon, and he wanted to learn the lay of that Basin land without delay. He had a chore to do that night, and he did not want to go it blind through the country.

Midafternoon had passed and he was still riding on. Cholla, stepping his borrowed pony through the shelter of mesquite and chaparral thickets, avoiding all traveled roads and ranch houses, had crossed the Comal and was heading toward the lower end of the Basin. The day had been uneventful. He had seen no man within hailing distance after Jeff Kuykendall had left him, and he had been on the move ever since the tall ranchman had given him the map.

Something after four o'clock found the Cholla Kid approaching Twenty Mile Flat, the home range of Puryear's K Breeching K spread. Among the men there were most likely some of those

161

who had murdered Sanna Merrill's father; who certainly had helped to pin that cowardly crime on Ace Sutton. Cholla's face was unyielding, savage with that thought ever before him. The ranch was still some distance away, about the proper distance, he judged, for him to reach it near twilight, as he desired.

The afternoon was stiflingly hot. Ugly clouds were piling up, spreading like smoke from a witch's cauldron. Copper-bellied and ominous they were, a sombre, bluish-green in color, shot through with a menacing light as the sun became obscured. The distant mutter of thunder came to Cholla's sharp ears, coming nearer and louder with each repetition. He saw a few fan-like, shivering flashes of lightning play above the hill crests, then they, too, were increasing in brightness and nearness as the cowboy came nearer to his goal. And as the afternoon lengthened toward sunset, an uncanny dark fell over ranch and plain and butte.

On a mesquite-covered rise not far from the K Breeching K ranch layout, as the unusually early twilight darkened the land, Cholla halted his pony. Ground-hitching him in the thick growth, he studied the place laid out before him. He surveyed it looking over the top of the big, unpainted, weather-beaten darkened barn that hunkered close to the ground like a giant bat with its wings spread.

The hacienda itself was weather-beaten also, but it had a strong look, built as it was of logs and adobe, as if it could withstand a siege. The bunk house stood near it, long and low. Its open door was not far from the kitchen of the hacienda, against the rear wall of which was piled firewood so high that it gave the impression that the inmates might be preparing for a long-holed-in sojourn and did not mean to be without hot-cooked grub.

Other small buildings on the usual ranch order were scattered about. Cholla recognized the blacksmith shop at once by its wide entrance from which came the occasional flashes of a flickering forge fire. There was an empty cow corral on one side of the big barn, and on the other the horse corral, filled now with vari-hued horses milling about, tossing their heads, snorting and sniffing, restless as are all ranch animals at the approach of a storm.

And all about, as far as Cholla's eyes could reach there were Puryear's broad rangeland acres, many of which had been filched from their proper owners as the man now wanted to filch the land belonging to Sanna Merrill.

Cautiously making his way from one cover of scrub to another, Cholla left the rise and approached the quiet looking layout. Not a soul was in sight, and it was in his mind to gain the inside of the hacienda without being discovered.

What he would do there, remained to be seen, but he wanted real cover for his job. If he could fort-up in the house—

He had almost reached a rear corner of the hacienda when he heard the muffled tapping of ponies' hoofs approaching from the northeast. At the same moment, he saw an overalled cowboy come out of the blacksmith shop with a piece of metal in his hand and walk to a nearby wagon.

The flashes of lightning were getting closer now, more ominous. Thunder was rolling with the nearness of the storm's approach. It was that and the shuffling of the horses' hoofs in the corral that had so far swallowed up any sounds that Cholla might have made. But he knew that discovery was imminent now. He could never make the door of the hacienda without being seen.

The swift glance he shot about him showed the high pile of wood his safest bet. Without a moment's hesitation he snaked behind it, crouching low, eyes glued to a crack between some piled logs. He was not ten feet away from the bench outside the bunkhouse where the punchers washed.

As he watched, two punchers rode up to the corral and dismounted, turning their ponies in the corral with the others when they had yanked off saddles and bridles. They carried the accoutrement inside the barn, with swift glances at the lowering sky and the lightning flashes, then came sauntering on to the bunkhouse. They stopped at the bench and poured water into two hand basins.

Cholla waited until their faces and hands were well lathered with soap before inching up from his covert, black butted .45 covering them steadily. Then his voice gritted out ominously:

"Grab sky, hombres, and grab it pronto!"

Making no move to lift their hands, the two riders grinned at each other from their soap covered features. And then, before Cholla could snap another command, a voice from behind him said:

"Easy, pardner! You're speakin' out o' turn."

Trapped! Cholla half twisted as logs rolled down and tumbled about his feet, his eyes shifting. A man with a ready rifle stood in the kitchen window, covering him, a grin on his hard face. The men at the wash bench calmly went on with their ablutions, their grins broader. And another dark-and-scarred-visaged puncher quietly stepped from the kitchen door, gun that glinted in the swift lightning flashes in hand. He also was grinning. Grinning, but not in friendliness. They had him cold turkey!

CHAPTER XIII

OPEN SEASON ON BREECHING K KILLERS

THE Cholla Kid managed to let loose one shot before he was heeled over backward against the side of the kitchen, stumbling and sprawling in the tumbled firewood. His last sight was of the burly man advancing from the kitchen, staggering from the smash of the bullet, as he dropped his gun. Then Cholla was grabbed roughly by the two young cowboys who leaped at him from the wash bench. He caught a lightning glimpse of the foremost one, not much more than an evil-eyed boy, as he came at Cholla with the .45 he jerked from his holster. He did not shoot, but the Cholla Kid went down as he was slashed on the head with the heavy gun butt.

"I'll kill him!" gritted the hatchet-faced youth. "Tryin' to hold me up like that, huh?"

But the wounded man, reeling and staggering up to Cholla, intervened.

"You won't do none of a such," he said thickly. "This is the big boss's say, Wiz." He balanced himself against the kitchen wall, breathing heavily as he ordered: "Truss him up and chunk him in the storeroom. And you, Poke, light a shuck for Hondo, storm or no storm. Tell the boss what's happened, and git Doc Somers out here pronto. Damn shootin' kioty got me through the lung, an' I'm bleedin' plenty inside . . . Wasn't lookin' for him to play so salty with us a-crackin' down on him."

"Tell the boss that this hombre Renfrow's done played his last tune," growled the man in the window. "An' I'm thinkin' us five is due for plenty jamboree when we divvy up that thousand *pesos* Puryear thought this vinagarroon's hide was worth."

The other youthful cowboy who had been at the wash bench, one they were calling Poke, a thin and wiry young puncher with rat eyes in his wizened, hard face, was bending over Cholla. Suddenly he jerked off Cholla's hat, bursting out with:

"Renfrow? Like hell his name's Renfrow! I could a'told you that right off if I'd been in Hondo the night he was bungin' up Zach Dagget! Renfrow? Say, I know this jigger. He comes from the Animas country in New Mex, an' his handle out there is the Cholla Kid. I've seen him afore—more'n once, too. He's a shore damn hellion, an' plenty wanted. Hell! Who'd a' thought it?"

"You shore o' that, Poke?" asked the wounded man weakly, as he inched forward to get a good look at Cholla's unconscious face. There was an evil glint in his pain-shot eyes.

"Shore as I'm standin' here!" Poke answered excitedly. "Yes, sir! An' it ain't been so long since I did see him, neither. Remember that trip lately when I sneaked back up into New Mex for—well, never mind. Guess you know, but anyway, I wasn't a-hangin' out none in Mobeetie, but spendin' my time in a sort o' Mex town not far from there, and this hombre come there a-hellin' one night, shootin' up the place to a fare-you-well—left a lot of 'em laid out, an' done for another sheriff, too. Leastways I can't say for shore whether the hombre croaked or not, 'cause I was kinda in a hurry gettin' back, but they's plenty want placards out for this shootin' fool, tacked up different places." He gave the unconscious Cholla a vicious yank as he helped the other cowboy pull him from the woodpile.

"Uh-huh." The wounded man laughed shortly— and the laugh ended in a gurgling cough.

With men on each side of him, half lifting, half dragging him along, with no sign of consideration in their handling, Cholla was bumped into the hacienda, through the kitchen, where the man at the window turned and followed them with his rifle in the crook of his arm, and on through a narrow hallway to a heavy door at its end. The rough handling did one thing for Cholla. The blow on his head with the gun butt had been a glancing one, and he came to his senses before the men carrying him were half way through the kitchen. He did not let his captors know, though, and so, darting brief glances as he was dragged along, he marked the route in his mind.

The two men thrust him inside the small room at the end of the passage while the other stood at the door on guard with his rifle. Then began a thorough job of binding him up. They bound his hands and ankles, slipping the riata which they used up about his neck and securing its other end to a beam in the unplastered ceiling, leaving him scant play. Any squirming or twisting on the prisoner's part would succeed only in drawing the noose tighter.

Satisfied, after carefully surveying their work, the renegades left him on the floor, booting him in the side once for luck before they left. The hatchet-faced youth snarled to his companion:

"When an' if he comes to right soon, Wiz, he's due for a surprise, findin' himself in one jam he can't git out of, the Cholla Kid can't."

Cholla held himself firmly in hand to keep from starting at the realization that he was known. That young puncher, whoever he was, must have recognized him during the few moments of unconsciousness. But it could make no dif-ference—now. Anything he had ever done in his life was picayunish compared with having killed Sheriff Newt Swinton, no matter how right he had been, no matter what his provocation. There could be no excuses to these men, and he knew they would be considered right in the eyes of a world who could not know the facts.

It was still more painful to contemplate that now he could not expect, by any wildest stretch of the imagination, any outside aid. Nobody who might have helped him had the faintest idea where he was. He had been distinctly advised to head for the hills, and here he had come the opposite direction—headed straight into trouble from which it looked as if he could not extricate himself.

He did not open his eyes until he heard the door slam and knew his captors had gone, leaving him in what they believed a deep, gun-butt-engendered sleep. He heard a heavy bar shoot into place outside the door. Then slowly he opened his eyes and looked around. The scrape of spurred feet receded to the kitchen.

He was in a store room, he saw at a glance, a place piled with a heterogeneous collection of miscellany of the sort that always piles up in ranch houses and is shoved into such an out-of-the-way place in case it should some day be needed. The supplies were kept here also, he saw when his eyes took in the high-piled cases of canned goods, the hams and sides of bacon hanging from the rafters.

There was one window in the place, but it was

barred. That meant that the owner of this hacienda probably sometimes had use for his own private prison for refractory gunmen. A place hard to get out of, that was sure enough, even if a man had the use of his arms and legs and didn't have his head in a noose. The Cholla Kid was bottled up more tightly than he had been in the Hondo jail.

Nothing like making a try to escape, though, and he got busy at once. His wrists were bound tightly together, as were his ankles, but thank all his gods, they had not wrapped the riata around his hands. His fingers were free—if that would be of any use. And it had to be!

Shoving his hands downward and arching his back, inch by inch, holding himself taut so that the riata should not tighten about his neck, he drew his legs up. By dint of hard straining, at last he was able to touch a boot heel, then with a thrill of triumph felt his fingers wrapping around it. Fumbling awkwardly with his bound hands, one of which was so much in the way, at last he was able to unscrew the boot heel, though the effort brought the sweat starting from every pore in his body.

Holding firmly to the loosened boot heel, from a riveted slot inside it he snicked down a short, sharp steel blade some inch and a quarter in length. It was a painful job, making use of every muscle in his hands, but in shorter time than might have been supposed, the hard-tied Mexican

172

knots in the riata, which would have resisted any amount of twisting and tugging, were severed. His hands free, only a few more slashes ripped through the riata around his chest and then, drawing a jack-knife from his pocket, he slashed through the rope around his feet. He was free! So far, at least, so good.

Screwing back the heel and thrusting the pieces of rope in a hip pocket, he stood up, making no sound, letting circulation flow back into the numbed members, then flung the loose noose from his neck. Looking about him, he searched the stacks of supplies, and the jumble of ranch and household oddments, looking for something he felt sure must be there.

The storm was nearly upon the ranch now, and the store room almost in pitch darkness save for the vivid flashes of lightning that streaked across the floor. The thunder cracked louder, but Cholla was glad of the sound which deadened any his movements might make. By the flashes of lightning, in a corner, resting on top of a salt pork box, he at last found what he sought.

It was a meat cleaver, heavy and rusted, but still a good weapon though past the days of its original use. The Chinese cook evidently used it now to open cans with. Cholla having seen such a thing put to like use before, had sought it out unerringly. Weighing it in his hand, he glided to the grilled window, glancing corral-ward.

The whole world lay in a greenish darkness now; the sky was boiling with clouds black as indigo. Birds were swiftly beating homeward, and the range animals were more restless, snorting more loudly, registering their fear and indignation at the performances of the elements. In the west the sunset, blotted out by the roiling clouds, stained their lighter edges like blood, and the scent of rain came on the brief, quick gusts of wind.

"She'll hit like a ton o' brick in a minute," Cholla observed, and jumped as a sharp crack of thunder came with a sudden zig-zag streak of instantaneous light. "Sufferin' polecats, she hit close that time!"

Another crack followed the first, almost on its heels, louder than the first, deafening in its artillery-like report that shook the hacienda to its foundations. The lightning that streaked down with it blinded him as its dazzle lit up the whole landscape. The sharp squeal of frightened horses came from the corral.

Cholla gazed out the window, scanning the big hay barn a moment, sure that he had seen aright even in that blinding flash. And what he saw—the curling smoke that was quickly rising, a licking flame that shot through the roof, sent him into immediate action. Not a moment to lose now, if he were in fact the first to see what that lightning had done.

Hoisting a box of canned beans from the stacks of grub, he slammed it down on the floor with a terrific clatter. Immediately came the high sing-song of the Chinese cook, answered by gruff voices.

Boots thumped on the hallway floor coming from the kitchen on the jump to see what had happened. A man coughed outside the store-room door, and Cholla heard the bar being raised. He waited beside it, tensed, weapon raised. But the Fates to which he had prayed were with him then, for it was at that exact moment that the outer kitchen door banged open, and racing footsteps pounded on the kitchen floor.

"Hey!" bawled a voice Cholla recognized as belonging to the man called Poke. "*Hey,* everybody! For Gawd's sake, hit the grit out here! The big hay barn's afire! Fire! Fire, I tell you!"

Bedlam broke loose in the hacienda. The Chink cook was screeching like mad; voices cursed and swore as there was a concerted rush for the outer door. Cholla, braced hard beside the store-room door, gripped his heavy cleaver and waited, taut as a fiddlestring. Would the hombre just outside the door, alone now as Cholla had hoped for him to be, have a look inside the room at his prisoner, or would he join the others in their rush outside?

The man hesitated, hand on the bolt which Cholla could hear moving slightly, listened a moment and swore harshly. In that moment

Cholla once again banged down the box of canned beans, leaped back to his vantage point. Another curse from outside, then the door was flung open, swinging inward.

Cholla recognized the man who appeared as the one who had so cleverly covered him with his rifle from the kitchen window a while ago. He stood in the narrow doorway, pistol in hand. The rusted steel blade of Cholla's weapon gleamed in another flash of lightning as he struck, struck savagely and surely. The blunt edge of the cleaver thucked against the man's skull with sickening force, and the squat *paisano* went down, the cocked gun in his hand going off and burying its slug in the floor as he fell.

In that same split second, with one swoop, the Cholla Kid had the gun in his own hand, had whirled, leaping through the door.

"What was that shootin', Turkey—" began the burly, scar-faced young busky Cholla had heard Poke call Wiz. He was charging into the kitchen, gun in hand. His eyes slitted instantaneously as he caught sight of Cholla, but in that same instant two shots merged into one smashing explosion. A bullet scorched Cholla's right cheek as he twisted and crouched. His own heavy slug, sent with satanic sureness, took Wiz just below his Adam's apple, driving him backward through the screen door, his warm, smoking Colt slipping from his hand. He fell loosely, with a rattling gurgle, to lay sprawled and limp just below the steps.

Cholla took one instant from his speed that meant life to swoop up his own two guns from the kitchen table where a beneficent Providence had allowed his captors to let them lie carelessly. Dropping them into their holsters, and swabbing the blood from his scorched cheek, he kicked open the screen door and loosed two shots from Turkey's gun in his hand at the staring punchers coming on the leap. He missed, and the men made a wild dive for shelter behind the shed, disappearing from sight.

In that split-second, death snatched at the Cholla Kid from behind. Reached for and missed him by a gnat's eyelash. It could not have been instinct, was more like that sharp sixth sense of his working for him subconsciously, but something suddenly made him duck and whirl. And as he moved, a smashing report sounded in the far door leading from the kitchen. Cholla felt the lick of the bullet's wake past his armpit. Its impact against the lintel of the door where he had stood one second before, himself sending out intended messengers of death, was not two inches from him. But even as it struck, he was twisting trigger.

Jake Deever, one of Puryear's worst bullies, though Cholla did not then know his name, even if he recognized him instantly as the heavy man he had plugged when they had caught him at the woodpile, was leaning against the jamb of the inner door, gasping, choking, as blood rattled up from his lungs. The front of his shirt was stained with blood, and a smoking gun dangled from his fist when Cholla whirled to shoot. The man's face was drawn and set, his eyes like red-hot coins. He had dragged himself from his bed, hearing the commotion, and only missed sending the Cholla Kid to Boot Hill by the margin of a hen's whiskers. But the Cholla Kid did not miss in return.

With red, fighting rage boiling through his blood, his shot, trued by the chilled steel of his eyes, went home—where Cholla had intended it should. Six inches above Jake Deever's belt buckle, the slug bored in.

"Open season on Breechin' K killin' hombres today!" grated Cholla.

He dodged further back from the door as a fusillade of shots, harmlessly sent from the distant, hiding punchers spent themselves in the floor and wall. He flung a glance at the sprawling dead man.

"Hope you and your *compadre*, Wiz, have a good time in hell, busky. Tell him that the boss will be along pronto."

Instead of hurling himself headlong through the kitchen door, Cholla turned and ran through the long hallway that cut through the length of the hacienda to the front porch. The big front door was open and he slipped through, crept to the end of the porch. After a swift survey, he dropped off onto the ground and broke into a weaving run toward an adjacent outbuilding flanking the bunkhouse.

A gun opened on him from behind the shed just in back of the kitchen, its bullet kicking up a jet of dust at his feet. He did not stop his zig-zag run as he whipped a slug at the shanty. A moment later, he flung himself around and behind the wooden shack toward which he had headed. Circling it, he peered around a corner toward the shed.

The flying hoofs of a horse came beating back to him between the thunder cracks. They came from behind the corral near the blazing barn. Then Cholla caught a glimpse of a rider racing up the Hondo road, saw his quirt flash down time after time, in the jagged flashes of lightning that had been having thunder accompaniment, thunder that had had its light echo in gun spurts. He saw the staggering leaps of the roweled pony, urged on as much by his fear of the electrical terror as by the cruel metal raking his flanks. The Cholla Kid's lips shut tight, as he nodded. No horse could keep up that pace for long through that storm, and it was a long way to Hondo.

The reddening reflection from the blazing barn in its ever-widening circle and the steady play of the lightning flashes made the rider plain to the cowboy from the Panhandle who was waging his battle single-handed. It was Poke, whom the fire and the fighting had delayed in getting on his way to town, according to the orders of the burly man who lay dead in the hacienda. The same Poke who had declared the man now crouching behind the outbuilding in the red reflection of flames to be the "wanted" Cholla Kid. Cholla smiled.

"Only one of 'em left at this openin' session now," he muttered. "All right pardner, it's a shoot-out between me and you." He straightened, tensed to leap into the open. "Here I come, busky—look out!"

He was half-crouched again as he left the protection of the shed and ran diagonally toward the wooden shack behind which his enemy, the puncher he had first seen coming out of the blacksmith shop, had taken cover. Behind the shack he had tossed the now emptied gun he had captured into the underbrush. Now, as he ran, with both of his own guns before him, he watched the corners.

He had a split-second view of a hatted head, and he loosed a shot at it. With a weird yell, the fellow dodged and flung into the open, his jaw dropped, mouth hanging loosely. There was no bravado any longer, only terror as he lifted his gun and fired wildly. But Cholla, weaving aside, got him.

CHAPTER XIV

THE PLOTTERS GET BUSY

SATURDAY in Hondo. Since early in the afternoon the town had been filling. By late afternoon the hitchracks around the plaza were crowded. The last day of the week was always one for excitement and revels, but there was more than the usual to attract riders to town this day.

The bushwhacking of Lynn Merrill, the killing of the sheriff and the escape of the unknown Renfrow from jail were savory morsels. The interring of the late Sheriff Newt Swinton had brought a big and curious crowd. The rites were all over before the threatening storm broke, however, and the crowd sifted back to the center of the town, ready for whatever the evening might bring.

The menace of the storm and the subsequent downpour had driven many of the citizens of Hondo home early, but it had not deterred visitors. Ranch hands and punchers, with *dinero* in their pockets, ready for relaxation after their week of hard work, were all set for whatever was offered. They cared not for the ill behavior of the elements. It would have taken more than lightning and thunder, or a deluge, to have kept them from the squatty little town with its dubious pleasures. It was Saturday, a change from ranch routine was indicated, and a good time.

Hardly more than time for lamps to be lighted and the Legal Tender was full. All the other saloons in the town were well patronized also, as were the spots in honkytonk town. As usual though it was Puryear's Legal Tender that was the most popular place, the center of the gayest activities.

Faro and chuck-a-luck, poker and crap games, were running full blast. The rear dance hall was well patronized and the laughter of men and women, the music of the string orchestra mingled with the more raucous shouts of the men in the bar room and about the gaming tables. The chink of checks was steady.

Creed Calkins, supposed proprietor, was himself behind the bar. Puffed up with his importance as newly appointed chief deputy sheriff under Putt Ratliff, acting sheriff by the orders of the big boss, Calkins had, however, put aside his official duties for the evening. He was attending strictly to raking in the freely spent *pesos* which passed over the bar.

Zach Dagget, once more able to be out and among his fellows, though showing signs of having been in an encounter, was present to aid Calkins if trade became too brisk. For the moment he was sitting at a table with Putt Ratliff and Boyce Puryear, talking.

As an obbligato to his monosyllabic remarks, Puryear, quite obviously not yet recovered from his recent spell of ill humor over the escape of Renfrow, was idly riffling a deck of cards, dealing himself imaginary poker hands. He appeared to have but slight interest in anything that was going on around him, though his keen eyes missed nothing.

His apparent indolence was jarred from him suddenly by a sound from outside. It was the clatter of a furiously ridden horse slithering to a stop before the saloon. The boss of Comal half rose to his feet, his hand unconsciously sliding to his thigh. It dropped on down as a drenched and mud-spattered rider lunged through the swinging green doors. The rider was Poke, puncher from the K Breeching K spread, and he was panting, his eyes staring about wildly as he strode in.

"Where's Puryear?" he demanded, his voice strident as his glance darted from bar to tables. "He here?"

The czar of Comal got to his feet, lips tightening. He stalked toward the hesitating cowboy.

"What's the row, Swanzy?" he asked sharply. "Want to see me about anything important?"

"Important?" echoed Poke hoarsely. "Gawdelmity! Lissen, Boss—"

"Hold it!" snapped Puryear, pitching down

183

his cards with a flip of his wrist. "Give this fellow a drink, Calkins, to get him over the dithers, then—" he jerked his head toward the private office behind the bar. "Come on in here, Swanzy."

The rat-faced Poke almost choked on the drink he swallowed at a gulp, his eyes bulging at Puryear calmly walking toward the office. With scores of curious eyes upon them, the owner of the K Breeching K walked on into his private sanctum. His panting puncher followed him down the bar and into the small room, closing the door behind him. After locking the door and seeing that the shades were drawn, Puryear lighted a stub of candle on the table in the center of the floor and turned to face Poke.

"Well, spit it out," he said sternly. "What's eating you?"

Poke did spit it out, jerkily and excitedly. He told of Cholla's coming to the ranch, of his capture and miraculous escape. He told of how the man from the Panhandle, on whom Boyce Puryear so desired to get his hands, had shot up the place, laying out Turkey, Wiz and Jake. He even put to Cholla's credit the firing of the barn to which the lightning itself had attended.

"Hell only knows what he done after I lit a shuck," Poke finished mournfully, with a wary eye on his boss as if he feared Puryear would blame him for the whole debacle. "I didn't wait to see, for I come straight here soon as I could catch up my pony that had gone hog wild in the corral like the rest of 'em—I come jest like Jake told me to. Though Gawd knows that poor hombre ain't never goin' to tell nobody nothin' any more—not since that rattler gun-fighter got through with him."

For minutes after Poke Swanzy finished his hurried, brief account, Boyce Puryear did not speak. He was shaken and came near to showing it. He held himself in check only by the firm knowledge that by giving way he would be lessening his hold on one of his own men whom he ruled by stern, harsh measures. This stranger from the Panhandle moved just a little too swiftly and was too deadly of purpose to suit him.

For a moment he fervently wished he had used other tactics with the man and had made him an offer to join his, Puryear's, own forces. The man who would be king had need of many just such men as Cholla Sutton had already proved himself to be. In so proving, though, he had laid out some of Puryear's best fighting men.

Four of them laid out! And his main hay barn gutted by fire! It was a jolting body blow. He was quite ready to believe, with Poke, that in some way Cholla had managed to get into the barn and fire it.

When Puryear did speak, it was to repeat what had been the burden of his remarks for hours.

"He's got to be caught," he said at last, his eyes hard as agates. "That's final; cold turkey. If you blithering idiots out there at the Breechin' K hadn't let him get away, he'd swing from the highest cottonwood in Hondo this very night. He's going to do that yet—if not tonight, before he's many hours older!" He glowered at Poke. "You keep what I say and what's happened out on the range to yourself, *sabe*? I'll do all the talking necessary for publication."

"Shore," blurted Poke, "but you don't know it all yet, boss, not by a dang sight. I got a good look at that jasper today when I knocked him cold. He ain't no stranger to me. Maybe his name is Ace Renfrow, like he says; maybe not. But out in the Animas an' Seven Rivers country west of New Mex's Pecos, he's known as the Cholla Kid—an' a heller if ever one growed!"

"Never mind the rest," clipped Puryear.

The real name of the Ace Renfrow who was bothering him, the hombre's antecedents, or what might have been his previous record was of no consequence to him just then. What was interesting him was the best way in which to put an end to the man's existence with all the expedition possible.

A forked vein was pounding in his forehead as he prowled about the small room. Viciously he hurled aside his chewed cigar, pawing in his pocket for a fresh one.

186

"Get on out and send Ratliff and Calkins in here to me," he snapped, as he suddenly stopped short. "And remember, Swanzy, one word out of you about any of this, and I'll skin you alive."

"I savvy," Poke muttered as he flung out the door. "Hell, I ain't plumb crazy, Boss!"

Poke Swanzy, puncher from the K Breeching K spread was not the only one who made a galloping trip into Hondo that late afternoon and early evening, regardless of the storm. And on as urgent business, though to the naked eye it would not appear so to be.

The reason for it was a hurried visit the Cholla Kid made to the nearby ranch of Jeff Kuykendall as soon as he had completed his one-man raid of Puryear's K Breeching K. Medicine talk that was made at once on his arrival resulted in some plans being changed; in others being put into action without delay.

Had Boyce Puryear possessed anything of a clairvoyant sense he would have known that some things were already beginning to happen right under his nose in the Legal Tender. Even before Poke Swanzy made his dramatic entrance with his more than disturbing dramatic story.

Red Blake, *segundo* of Kuykendall's Bar Lazy 3 Slash stood near the rear end of the long bar, draped loosely across the rail, a glass of whiskey in front of him. His eyes were half closed, and he weaved rather unsteadily at his stance. He was flanked by two convivial companions whose voices ever and anon were raised in song.

At a hitch rail on the street outside, some distance down from the Legal Tender, three winded, foam-flecked and mud-covered ponies may have shown evidence of the dash that had been made through the dark, riding hell bent in an effort to reach town before Poke Swanzy should get there, cutting across range to gain miles on him, but the men at the rail were as devil-may-care as though there was nothing in the world of interest but the drinks in front of them on the bar; the noise and excitement around them. The trio were evidently out to make a night of it.

None of them appeared to take the slightest notice of Poke Swanzy as he came out of the back room and whispered in turn to Calkins and Ratliff, nor did they appear to observe that Calkins and Ratliff quickly made tracks for the private sanctum. They only called for more drinks—and more. So many, in fact, that it was not long afterward that the two buckaroos with Blake led him out of the saloon seemingly much the worse for liquor (most of which was at that moment sloshing around in a spittoon at the bar rail), and earnestly coaxing him to come along and sleep it off.

So ordinary was such an occurrence that scant attention was paid to the three when they left the

Legal Tender. They wove their way across the plaza toward the Medina House, the same two-storied adobe hotel building where the Cholla Kid had registered on his first night in Hondo. In the lobby, Red Blake's two friends halted with him. They dumped him unceremoniously into a chair near the end of the clerk's desk while they arranged with old man Phillips for a room.

While his two companions were attending to this, Blake sprawled drunkenly in the chair. The clerk had his back turned toward his uninteresting intoxicated guest, the worthy Phillips being far more interested in the business at hand and in the small gossip offered by the two cowpunchers. He chimed in as they made comments on the happenings in the town in the last few eventful hours.

Armed with the key the clerk handed out to them, Blake's *compadres* walked back to him finally and took him to his room, with difficulty dragging him up the stairs. Old Phillips grinned a toothless grin of understanding and sympathetic commiseration. He had a chaffing word or two for the cowboys when they came back presently, announcing that they were headed for the pleasure resorts of the town. The night was still too young for them to turn in. Blake could sleep off his drunk alone.

The old clerk below, nodding in his tipped-back chair, would have been considerably surprised and puzzled had he known that only some fifteen minutes after the two punchers had departed, how busy Red Blake got of a sudden. Making no noise he got up from the bed in the darkened room and made his way to the door. Warily he opened it, and after a cautious survey of the deserted passage, he knotted a polka-dot bandanna about the outer door knob. Then he ducked back inside.

Chuckling to himself, the *segundo* lighted the lamp, placed it on a table near his bed, shucked off his boots and settled himself to read an old magazine that he'd salvaged that afternoon and shoved into a hip pocket for emergencies. With Durham sack, brown papers, a pile of matches and a pint of liquor within reach, he proceeded to relax and take life easy for an indefinite period.

For a man who had so recently been helplessly drunk, he had become cold sober in remarkably quick time. . . .

CHAPTER XV
THE GOOSE HANGS HIGH

BY NIGHTFALL, the storm had reached the point of almost hurricane proportions. Punchers riding early into Hondo missed the worst of it. As it grew later, instead of abating, the rain and wind and lightning which had struck across the range land like a fury about the time Ace Sutton's guns were working in unison with it, increased.

It could not deter the Cholla Kid. He stopped in the Kuykendall hacienda, after Jeff's three punchers had ridden away at top speed, only long enough for a breathing spell and some hot grub, then he was off again. He, too, headed for Hondo. Another chore awaited him there. On the success of the mission much depended— for every honest rancher in the community. For Sanna Merrill his success would mean triumph over her enemies. And Cholla's own life chances would be advanced in no small degree.

In the night blackness, closely wrapped in a borrowed black poncho, since his own still reposed in Grumbles' livery barn, he drifted along west of Hondo to reach the town by a circuitous route. The storm was raging in full force, accompanied by rain, driving sheets of it. The devil's own night—black as the pit of hell, raw, chilling; rain that beat against the rubber of poncho searching out where it could run rivulets inside of neckline and up sleeves—a rain not warm as might have been expected in that semi-tropic land, but chill as if swept down on icy blasts, cutting into the marrow of bones, stinging Cholla's face like a thousand pricking needles.

But oddly enough, with his brain heated beyond fever point, the rider felt no unusual cold as he went on and on through the increasing storm that swept across the Basin to the howling tune of a banshee wind, sending horses and cattle to shelter, scurrying coyotes and gray wolves to their holes.

Only the lone rider who was the Cholla Kid seemed to be abroad in the inky, wind-swept night—forging on and on, sloshing across marshy flats, circling to the bare ridges of benchland through mile after mile of stinging, haunting, eerie blackness. Thoughts were in his fevered brain, none of them regret for the dead men he had that afternoon left behind him. They were bitter, biting thoughts of more he had that night learned of evil plots to turn out homeless, wanderers, Sanna Merrill and others in the valley who had dared to defy the mandates of Boyce Puryear and his brutal-hearted, land and cattle-grabbing men. And Cholla had with him a memory of the firm handclasp and whispered words of thanks and encouragement from a blue-eyed girl who knew he was doing his best. That urged him on to supreme endeavor.

Drenched to the skin, mud-spattered and sodden, he pushed on through a black, storm-ravaged universe, his way illumined by zigzag lightning flashes. Sliding, slithering through long, unexpected stretches of mud, down slimy slopes into the sinister black pits of rocks and water, searching out a way that should not allow him to approach the squatty town by any known road. Holding his bronc by main force from falling, rain-lifting him from scrambling, riding in his stirrups.

Cholla did not seem to know that far back along the road a sharp gust of wind had caught his sombrero and sailed it far out into the black-ness so that his raven-black hair was dripping with rain and shining in the intermittent electric flashes. Nor that the poncho, whipped by the same wind and the pounding rain was fast being torn to ribbons.

The wind, moaning and whining, drove gusts and sheets of water before him, slashing at man and pony. A hell of a night. But always and ever he pushed on—on toward Hondo, grim and ruthless. For the Cholla Kid had declared war. It *was* that now, to the hilt, or until every man in Hondo or belonging to the K Breeching K spread who was responsible for Lynn Merrill's dry-gulching, for Sanna's grief and pain, and for Cholla Sutton's himself being made a murderer in defense of his own life should have been forced to pay the price in full.

As far as he could see when at last the twinkling lights of the town, blurs through the pouring rain, apprised him that he was coming into it from in back of some adobe shacks, there was no one abroad in the streets. Cholla's lips tightened with satisfaction. He had hoped for that. It might be the devil's own night, but it was one most positively made to the Cholla Kid's purpose.

He staked his horse in the lee of an abandoned shack near those adobe huts on the edge of town and went on afoot, but at no time taking to the streets. Sifting through the blackness back of the scattered string of false fronts and squatty shacks, he went on until he reached the two story Medina House, with the lights of the Legal Tender saloon shining across the street through the pouring rain.

Gaining the rear of the hotel, Cholla drew one of his six-shooters from beneath his poncho and carefully cleaned the mud and water from it. Seeing to it that the weapon was fully loaded, as well as his other gun that had not been looked to since the late afternoon, he considered the best way to enter the place unobserved. He cast an eye toward the slanting roof of the porch from which he had dropped on his first visit to the place, but it was wet and slippery now. Small chance for hand- or foothold if he should shin up a porch post to catch the edge. He shook his head. That way must be attempted only if there were no other.

Cautiously he slipped along the rear of the place, noiselessly trying doors, windows. The door of the center hall opened at his touch, creaking a little, but with patience he inched it open far enough to admit his tall, husky body, eased himself through it into the dim hall and then tiptoed up the back stairway.

A wall lamp burned low in the upper hallway, and at its end the front staircase led to the lobby below. Cholla caught a glimpse of the unsuspecting old Phillips, his head sunk low on his chest as he drowsed and waited for his guests to return from their merrymaking so that he could close up for the night and do some real sleeping. Cholla smiled. Darn well protected, that hotel.

Moving with cat-like caution, he scanned the flanking rows of doors with their big black-painted numbers. Presently he found what he sought—one on whose knob was knotted a bandanna handkerchief. Softly he rapped upon the panels with his raw wet knuckles—a pre-arranged signal, one rap; two short ones—and a moment later Red Blake opened the door a crack and squinted out. With a grin he motioned the wet, bedraggled and muddied Cholla to enter.

"You got here sooner than I'd thought you would," Blake whispered when the door was noiselessly closed. "You must a' done some tall ridin' through a storm like this. Hell of a night."

Cholla nodded shortly. "All o' that, Blake," he whispered back, "but I'm thankin' Mr. Storm King for it." He glanced sharply at the bootless cowboy. "You got it?"

Blake grinned and nodded, as he stuck his hand into his pocket, pulled it out with something in it. His whisper was still lower as he gave the Cholla Kid some quick, additional information. Five minutes later, Cholla slipped cautiously out of the door, and moved up to the hall to the last room, one which overlooked the plaza.

Inserting the duplicate key from old Phillips' cherished ring of pass keys which Blake had filched from the key rack downstairs an hour ago while he was doing his job of acting drunk for the old clerk's benefit, and as his companions had arranged for his room, Cholla unlocked the door of Boyce Puryear's darkened room and let himself in. The Yale spring lock clicked to after him. A flash of lightning showed him the time as it shot across the dial of Puryear's small alarm clock, ticking away on the washstand. Earlier than Cholla had supposed, for he felt that he had spent hours in the saddle coming through that storm. Only about half past nine. Oh, well, he would have a little time for getting a rest and a breathing spell. He needed it.

When Puryear finally clumped up the front stairs and along the hall, flinging back a grumpy good-night to the obsequious old clerk, it was almost twelve o'clock. The storm had not abated, the howl of the wind and the rain slashing across the window panes almost blotting out the clomp of feet in the hallway, and the muffled voices. Shaking the rain from his slicker outside his door, the czar of Comal rumbled a good-night to a couple of his gun men bodyguards. They were always at his side, and occupied a room across the hall from his. He fumbled in his pocket for his key.

Unlocking his door, he stepped inside and closed it, letting the lock fasten with a click. He struck a match, shielding it with his palm as he raised the chimney of a lamp and lighted it. A slight sound behind Boyce Puryear made him whirl around suddenly, his hand going to his hip in the manner of a man who lives in the constant shadow of death or reprisal, and with gun ready.

But his hand stopped halfway when—he looked into the muzzle of a Colt, held steadily in the hand of a man who stepped silently out of the clothes closet! A man wearing a black poncho on which drops and streaks of rain still glistened, and with a black neckerchief covering his face below his eyes—still gray eyes which glittered

197

ominously from beneath Red Blake's floppy sombrero—moved toward him swiftly, silently, and with terrible deadliness.

"Get 'em up!" rasped a low voice. "And the first yap out of you means a slug through your heart, Puryear. Stand just where you are."

Puryear gasped, swallowed—and obeyed.

Cholla worked rapidly and in silence, though few sounds could have been heard above the wind's loud wailing. Ripping open Puryear's shirt, he thrust a hand inside, loosened the clasp he had felt sure he would find there. While a low chuckle of triumph at his discovery rumbled in his throat, he gave a tug and whipped out a money belt.

His gun still unwaveringly covering the rancher and political boss, he turned the money belt over, examining it closely.

The rumble of triumph turned to a snarl of low-voiced rage at what he saw. In the yellow light of the lamp, Cholla could make out the dim initials L.C.M., and under them the Rafter M brand burned into the leather. Looking hard at Puryear while the big man's face was purpling to the explosive point in his rage and sense of being trapped, Cholla laughed—a short brittle laugh.

"Maybe you can explain how come you happen to be totin' around Lynn Merrill's money belt, eh, Puryear?" he drawled, with a contemptuous sneer.

"Who are you and what do you want?" Puryear demanded in a hoarse whisper, not daring to raise his voice. He was in a jackpot and he realized it full well. His eyes were darting about desperately, past the masked man and toward the door and windows. If he could just attract the attention of his two henchmen across the corridor—

Cholla saw the glances and interpreted them correctly. He gave another cold, low laugh. His hand tightened on his gun-butt as it was levelled still more menacingly. Puryear, his big shoulders drooping flabbily, understood. He brought his gaze back to the marauder, and stared into the steely gray eyes.

"Who'm I? I might be Jesse James or Billy the Kid—but I'm not," Cholla said grimly. "I reckon you know me without any special introductions, Puryear, and just about can guess the reason I'm here . . . You can't get away with murder all your life, hombre, and not run across somebody yearnin' to make you do a little payin' . . . Turn around," he jerked, "and put your hands behind your back."

"You damned murderin' rattlesnake!" Puryear gritted, but he obeyed the Cholla Kid's orders. There was something in the eyes of steel that showed him plainly that sudden death awaited him if he hesitated. "I'll get you for this! I'll have your hide staked—"

Cholla said shortly, as he got busy: "I reckon you're forgettin' one little point in all that threatenin' of yours, polecat . . . There's a recipe they tell about that goes somethin' about first catch your rabbit. I'm plumb willin' for you to go ahead—if you and your hellions *do* catch me before I'm ready to officiate at your own hangings."

Whipping lengths of pigging string from his belt, Cholla deftly rawhided Puryear's wrists together, taking a note from his own book in his own recent tying, and fastening the man's hands together also, palm to palm. With a violent shove he thrust him onto the bed, and performed the same operation on the man's ankles and feet, after shucking off his high-heeled, muddied boots.

Then taking a length of riata from beneath his poncho, Cholla proceeded to bind Puryear thoroughly with a series of half-hitches that started at his neck and worked down to his ankles. As a finishing touch he yanked off the neckerchief of the boss of the K Breeching K and stuffed it into the big man's mouth, tying it beneath his head. He paid no attention to Puryear's too-small black eyes that gleamed at him murderously, except by a grim chortle.

"Pretty neat, Puryear," the Cholla Kid remarked, standing back to survey his work. "Maybe so you'll do some thinkin' before

200

mornin'. There's plenty comin' to you—and quite some prayin', too—if you think that'll get such as you anywheres."

Leaving the big man helpless on the bed, Cholla walked calmly over to the lamp and pulled out the money belt he had stuffed in his pocket. Deliberately he took out the sheaf of bills inside it and carefully counted them. There were five thousand dollars exactly. He shot a cold glance at the trussed man.

"Three hundred dollars missin' here, Puryear," he snapped. "Won't stop for it now, but I'll maybe be comin' back to collect it. That will go quite a ways towards payin' for a certain funeral you're responsible for."

Shoving money back into the belt and the belt back into his pocket, Cholla calmly blew out the lamp, moved cautiously to the door, and slipped out of the room. He let the Yale lock click shut behind him, and cat-footed down the hall. Again stopping at Red Blake's door, he knocked, and slipped in when the *segundo* opened it on his darkened room. He stopped only long enough to whisper his luck, to gulp a drink and to return the key to Blake. Sometime during the night the *segundo* would sneak downstairs and restore the key ring, leaving it in some place that would lead Phillips to believe he had misplaced it himself. The old man would not mention a thing like that.

Warmed and fortified by the big slug of Red's liquor, Cholla sifted down the rear stairs and let himself out into the night.

"You won't lose your *rancho* now, Miss Sanna," he was saying to himself as he slipped off through the unabated downpour of rain toward where he had left his pony. He grinned wryly. "And I expect Jeff Kuykendall *et al* will be plum interested in what I've got to tell 'em *manana*." He chuckled as he drew his tattered poncho about him, unworried about the night ride that lay ahead of him through the storm. "Yes, sir, the goose is shore beginnin' to hang high!"

Kneeling on the floor before the window of her bedroom, her head at times hidden in the crook of her arm, at others lifted to glance out at the blackness and the storm, Sanna Merrill mentally followed the Cholla Kid every inch of the way of his journey that night, as he went about his reckless mission. Sometimes her eyes, bright with tears now, in the privacy of her own room, were lifted, trying to pierce the darkness as she looked out toward the rise behind the hacienda where was her father's newly-made grave. She could not see it, but she shivered as she knew how the rain was beating down upon it, the wind wailing a dirge that had its echo in her heart.

In that heart of the blue-eyed girl was the most fervent prayer of her life—a plea to her God and to the father who must be looking down on her from the weeping sky—for the success of the Cholla Kid in his search for Lynn Merrill's murderers. And for Ace Sutton's own safe return.

CHAPTER XVI
SUNDAY ON THE RANGE

SUNDAY was a real day of rest for the Cholla Kid. He had earned it. Long before daylight, after a ride through mud and rain and stormy wind he had again stealthily arrived at the ranch of Jeff Kuykendall, from which he had gone forth to Hondo hours before.

All was quiet about the ranch when he arrived, the silence of a ranch outfit hunkered down to outlast inclement weather. Splashing through the mud, the Cholla Kid rode up to the barn. With a tired sigh he got from his horse, and stabled the claybank. He gave a regretful thought to his own mount, back in Grumbles' livery barn, as he slapped a pat of thanks on the rump of the sturdy pony that had carried him through the night, hoping it would not be long now before once again he could feel the red and white streak that was understanding Jerky between his legs.

Jeff Kuykendall had not waited up for him, purposely. But a trusted employee was awake and waiting to attend to Cholla's wants. There was no need to take chances at this stage of the game, was Kuykendall's idea. It was only too likely spies were abroad, and with the price Cholla had on his head and with Puryear's determination to get rid of him at all costs, they must all move warily. It was even possible that one of the Bar Lazy 3 Slash riders was drawing pay from Puryear. There was need for caution on Cholla's part in arriving at the ranch. There must be no advertisement that the Cholla Kid was a guest beneath its hacienda roof.

Thankfully the weary cowboy turned in when Kuykendall's puncher led him to a room. He was glad for another chance to rest between sheets.

He was sleeping soundly when men were stirring about the ranch, and plans for Sunday were being made. At breakfast, eaten by lamp-light, Kuykendall announced that those of his men who wanted to might take the day off. There were pleased grins at the permission, and shortly afterward the place had a deserted appearance as groups of riders jogged away, shaved and dressed in their best, going their separate ways for a Sunday holiday.

The rain had stopped except for a drizzle, but dawn broke blustery, bleak and nasty, lighting a world of slaty clouds and drenched earth. But it did not deter Sanna Merrill from keeping her prearranged date and riding over to the Lazy 3 Slash. She arrived before midmorning to take dinner and spend the day.

Unaccustomed to sleeping past the time when the sun should by rights be high, Cholla, in spite of his weariness at the time when he turned in, which had made him believe he could sleep the clock around, was up and about long before Sanna's arrival. The imminence of that very event may have had much to do with his not sleeping any longer. It most surely did with the care he took in "sprucing up" with borrowed razor and comb.

Except for three or four entirely trusted cow punchers, the ranch was deserted when Cholla strolled out on the porch after a hearty breakfast, and looked about him. It was the first time he had been given an opportunity for studying the Kuykendall spread in the daylight and it impressed him, made him feel a little homesick.

The Kuykendall hacienda, and its surroundings, in spite of the fact that Jeff had long been a widower and that what feminine touches there were about the place were reminiscent of a woman's hand that had long been gone, reminded him—as Cholla's own home in New Mexico had always reminded him—that a love of poetry and peace had been an elementary essential in the hearts of the old-time cowmen. It was with all natural born cowmen. Though circumstances might force them to live with hands on guns, their homing instinct was true. Their love of peace was not expressed in words, but by the valiant way in which they fought for it, as the men of Blanco Creek were willing to fight for it now, as Sanna Merrill's father had battled for it to his death. And their poetry was not that on any printed page, but was shown in the settings of their haciendas and their surroundings.

Jeff Kuykendall's spread was a true ranch home that spoke of peace and contentment. There was a home feeling all about the place, even with the mist hanging heavily over alfalfa and deep, lush range land.

From the porch, the Cholla Kid looked out over spreading lands. A green valley sloped away to meet the hills. Green woods near the foothills showed mistily silver. The creek that tumbled not far away was swollen now from the night's rain, tossed with little foam-crested waves.

The hacienda, set in cottonwoods, was built of logs and adobe. A sort of ell had been fenced in by wire, and in that enclosure was still the evidence of a woman's hands in the flowers that struggled to flaunt their beauty through the weeds that tried to crush them out—neglected flowers now, once planted by Jeff's wife.

The Cholla Kid's eyes swept appreciatively over the layout. Just such a place as he had always dreamed of some day owning himself, with a girl (she would have blue eyes and a brave uplift of gold-brown head) who would work busily in a garden, sending the weeds to the perdition they merited.

He was thinking of that when he lifted his head to see approaching the girl who was in his mind—and in his heart. Sanna Merrill waved him a greeting as she came on, accompanied by Kip Helm. Even at the distance Cholla could see her wistful smile. He approved her bravery in coming, knowing how she must realize that only a few short days before it had been her father who had accompanied her on her Sunday visit to Jeff Kuykendall's ranch, a trip they had made weekly. She had come today, of course, to talk business—serious matters would be discussed at the Slash 3—but for the first moment of seeing Sanna, the Cholla Kid did not remember business. He could think only of her.

Sanna dropped from her mare lightly and Kip Helm led the spirited animal away. Smiling a little sadly, she came toward the porch steps, lithe and lovely in her riding breeches and shirt, with her poncho thrown back. Cholla's heart thumped oddly at the sight of her. Her hand was outstretched as she neared him.

"I don't need to ask," she said quickly. "I can read your eyes. You have something to tell me!"

Cholla nodded as he held her hand for a moment.

"Maybe, Miss Sanna," he said. "Leastways I don't think you're goin' to lose your Twin

Springs, but—" He stopped and laughed a little bashfully. "Maybe we'd better wait till we get into conference with Jeff and Kip—we've got right considerable medicine talk to make."

Sanna did not urge. She only said: "It's good to see you here and all right—so good. It—it gives me courage—knowing what you faced last night, and that you came back to tell about it."

"It wasn't nothin'," said Cholla. He did not expatiate, for he was too busy looking at Sanna Merrill.

His eyes took her in as she stepped on the porch, shaking her head to whip off the raindrops when she took off her wide sombrero. He leapt to help her as she slipped the poncho over her head. Lovelier than ever, he thought her to be. He had before seen her only at night, except in that one instance on the day of his arrest, when her grief for her father of necessity had made her white-faced and wan.

Cholla Sutton's gray eyes said unspoken volumes—his opinion of this slip of a girl whose head, with its damp, golden-brown ringlets clustering about her tanned face would come not far above his heart. That head would fit well into the hollow of his broad shoulder. Sanna's eyes were bluer than ever, he thought, wistful as they smiled bravely at him through mist-drenched lashes—eyes that a few days ago had held only sparkling life and joy. Now, through the machinations of the devil the Cholla Kid was determined to crush, all the girl's bravery could not quite hide the pain in their blue depths.

There was no doubt that Sanna Merrill was glad to see the Cholla Kid. Her trusting smile showed that when he took her hand in his firm clasp. And to Cholla, the girl with the wild-rose bloom whipped into her cheeks by the stinging mist that still hung damply on them, was the stuff that a man's dreams are made of. There was the look in his eyes that comes to a man when he is looking at the one girl in the world!

The full realization of that made him speechless for minutes; awkward. She was murmuring a few words about the matter which had once more brought them together. Startlingly he brought her away from that when he finally spoke.

"Miss Sanna," he said soberly, though there was a small dancing glint in the depths of his eyes, as he still held to her firm brown hand, "there ought to be a law."

She smiled a little wearily, and with a sidewise tilt of her head looked up at him.

"A law?" she repeated. "Cholla, what good do you think *any* laws that we not already have could do for us?" Her tone was bitter. "In this country it's beginning to look as if laws were made only for the strong."

Cholla shook his head and grinned. "I'm not talkin' about that," he said firmly. "I'm talkin' about there should be a law against—against—"

"Against what, Cholla?" she asked, her blue eyes widening.

"Well, if you've got to have it," Cholla said, with something of his old careless recklessness, "there ought to be a law against you."

"Against *me?*" She jerked her hand away, staring.

"Uh-huh." Cholla was getting more sure of himself. "What I mean is somebody ought to make a law against anything as beautiful as you runnin' around loose on the ranges."

For the first time in many hours, Sanna smiled.

"Nice," she said, her voice low. "I might have expected a man like you to be a master of flattery, Cholla."

"It's not flattery," said Cholla, more solemnly. "It's Gawd's truth, and maybe you know it."

The appearance of Jeff Kuykendall in the doorway put an end to further persiflage. But all through the typical Texas ranch Sunday dinner that followed, Sanna was conscious that the eyes of the Cholla Kid were following her with dog-like devotion. He was trying to get through to her their message.

More important matters than personal opinions engrossed them at once—as soon as Jeff had led them into his big living room with its wide fireplace, its photographs and few etchings, its mementoes of the chase, and the now somewhat bedraggled chintz curtains which his wife had once hung in place. As soon as they were seated, Jeff Kuykendall's first observation was:

"You ain't goin' to lose your land, Sanna, thanks to Cholla here. But there's plenty more to do before we get down to bed rock o' provin' just who done for your paw." He turned to the cowboy. "Cholla, show Sanna what you corralled offen that skunk Puryear last night."

Sanna's lips trembled when she first saw the well-remembered money belt, but when both men insisted that she count the money that Cholla had salvaged from Boyce Puryear, and then she realized that she had in her hands the even five thousand dollars that meant she could do that thing which her father had tried to do, and in the trying had given his life, her eyes were misty. She looked up at Cholla and said evenly:

"Why are you doing all this for me, Cholla? Why run all these awful risks? My fight against Puryear is nothing to you."

"It's plenty to me, Miss Sanna," the Cholla Kid answered briefly, as their eyes clashed.

Jeff Kuykendall, seeing the interplay, glanced surprisedly from one to the other of them, then got up from his chair and strolled across the room, stopping to gaze at a photograph on the mantelpiece.

The Cholla Kid went on hastily, his voice lowered: "Some time maybe I'll get the right to tell you just how much it is to me—right now you don't know enough about me for me to do anything else but tell you that I'm here because I aim to see that you get your rights. And don't forget—those same people who're waitin' to do you out of 'em were, and still are, tryin' to job me for your dad's murder! I'm not takin' that layin' down. Think I said a little somethin' like that once before."

Kip Helm came in then, and Jeff Kuykendall turned from the contemplation of his wife's picture and whatever visions of past romance it may have evoked. Something in the unconscious glances between Sanna Merrill and the Cholla Kid had stirred those memories.

With Kip's appearance, the conversation became general; impersonal. They made no further mention of the serious subject which was uppermost in their minds until dinner was over and once again the three were in the big living room.

Kuykendall, Sanna, Kip and the Cholla Kid settled down then for a real council of war. Boyce Puryear would have been vastly surprised—and alarmed, before they were finished—if he could have had a listening ear at the keyhole.

When all business, all plans had been discussed, and there remained only the waiting for the passage of the hours which must elapse before plans could be carried out, Sanna and Cholla, slickered and booted, went for a cautious stroll west of the hacienda. Walking along the banks of the creek, as they further discussed their affairs in low tones, Sanna confided, more than she had before, in the man from the Panhandle.

"There's something brewing among my father's friends, Cholla," she said quietly. "I'm sure of it. Uncle Kirk, from the Clover Leaf, Bart Lacey—you already know him and how fine he is—Mike Groce, another of the Blanco Creek real men, and lots of others, as well as close-mouthed Jeff Kuykendall, have something up their sleeves. They don't want me to know about it, and they don't even guess that *I* guess. They won't tell me a thing when I try to ask questions, try to dig something out of them, and even men like Jeff and Kip, my own foreman, are evasive when I pry. Kip knows about it, of course, and his attempts to lie are amusing—if there's anything left in this dreary old world that can be amusing. I don't know—I'm only guessing of course—but what I think is that they suspect who killed and robbed Dad, and mean to do something about it. Not," she added, so bitterly that a new rage surged in Cholla's heart against the man he had tied up the night before, "that I, that any of us, don't know already who was the instigator of it . . . The thing to do is to prove who were the actual killers, and some way I've an idea they *know!*"

"You think so?" asked Cholla sharply.

She nodded, and her eyes turned from him to look out wearily over the misty rangeland. "I don't know how they found out—have not the faintest idea. God only knows what it's going to mean. Range war—if nothing worse. But I can't learn a thing from anybody—they won't tell me. I do know, though, that if their suspicions of who were the killers becomes a conviction, that they will act pronto, Cholla."

Cholla drew a long breath and nodded soberly in return.

"Yeah, it's pretty near a show-down," he admitted, in an uneasy mutter. For a moment or two he was silent, thinking deeply, before he lifted his head and squared his shoulders. "Reckon I'll have to call off this plumb scrumptious day an' get on the prod again, Miss Sanna."

Sanna put out a hand abruptly and let it press on his arm.

"I know, Cholla," she said softly. "I know . . ." There was tender pleading in her blue eyes as she looked up at him, a sigh coming from her heart. "I—I haven't told you—I ought to . . . But—but you're a pretty good rock to lean on, Cholla Kid, and never in my life have I felt so much like leaning." She gave a quick, determined laugh, and her bravery was again uppermost. "But don't think I'm going to be any moss on the rock, Cholla . . . I'm going to do all that *I* can—every-

216

thing!—only I'm hoping *you'll* let me know what it is, if the others will not."

"Shore," said the Cholla Kid, but he did not dare look into her eyes. Then he said quickly: "I reckon there ain't any use o' me tryin' to tell you how much I've enjoyed this day, Miss Sanna— just bein' here with you, as if there wasn't anything else, any trouble in the world. It's been the most wonderful day I reckon I've ever known, in spite of everything, all our troubles, and all that . . . All I wish on this old earth is that I could be certain there would be other such days, that there would shore be some tomorrows, like the same, and that's cold turkey."

"Same goes for me," replied Sanna softly, but her own blue eyes were veiled so that he could not look into their depths. Then she looked up quickly. "And listen, Cholla, I can't tell you my feelings in regard to your help in this mess, but I want you to know this: If you're fighting for me, I'm fighting for you, shoulder to shoulder. We're pardners, aren't we?"

"Thanks," said Cholla, with heart pounding so that he did not recognize his own muffled voice. "Shore we are. And—and—sometime Sanna, maybe—sometime when you know all about me more'n you do now—when maybe you can apologize for a fool that didn't know they was honest to God people and things in the world and just went on a-hellin' till—Well, maybeso I can say—" He turned suddenly and gripped her hand, pulling her along with him toward the hacienda. "Aw, hell, pardner! I got to light a shuck. Plenty doin'—come on!"

CHAPTER XVII

PURYEAR STARTS
RANGE JUMPING

IF THAT Sunday had been a day for Cholla Sutton to remember in the winter of his old age, the same could not be said for Boyce Puryear. He would remember it all right, and the Saturday night that preceded it, but with thoughts that would be far from pleasurable. Not only had he suffered pain of body at the hands of the Cholla Kid, but what was worse, his dignity had been offered incurable injury.

He had not been discovered until well after daybreak, and he had really suffered physically during the age-long night before his guards, worried because no sounds came from his room in answer to their knocks, had finally broken in the door. Cholla's Mexican knots had not been kind to the big man's tortured body. The Panhandle cowboy had not intended them to be. Puryear could at first only fume the rage that his dried tongue could not speak.

After coffee and some good whiskey had been brought to him, he was finally able to manage a little breakfast. That over, he went into a council of war with some of his most prominent and trusted henchmen who were hastily summoned.

"It was the Cholla Kid who did this thing to me, of course," he croaked. "I'd have known him anywhere, mask or no mask. I'll get that rattler, if it's the last thing I ever do on this earth! Plain killin' or hangin' is a mile too good for him. I'll have him skinned alive and nail his cursed hide on the Rafter M ranch house, by hell! And what's left will be staked on an ant hill!"

"We'll get him, Boss," assured Putt Ratliff, as his heavy jaws clamped down.

He gave the boss of Comal a jerked signal that he wanted to have a little medicine talk with him in private. When Puryear had sent his other men outside the room, Putt, his sheriff's star shining importantly, pulled up a chair and talked close to his head man's ear. A mixture of emotions spread across Puryear's heavy face as his fore-man talked.

"Listen, Boss," Ratliff said in a lowered tone. "I got a plan to smoke out that lone wolf, and just you listen to it all first before you shut me up. Might be, too, some other folks would be seein' quite a few things more your way before it's all over and done with, at that—" He leered meaningly. "If nothin' else, you'd be gettin' good an' even on more'n the Cholla Kid. It's this: I figger from the way things have been breakin' that there's more'n a little in that talk about this side-winder from the Panhandle bein' stuck on Merrill's gal." Puryear's face darkened at the mention of Sanna's name, but Ratliff ignored that and hastened on. "Now, here's what we could do. We'll grab that gal, and if the Cholla Kid's anywheres around, it'll bring him a-hellin' to rescue her. Savvy the burro?"

He did not mention that while Sanna was in custody that it would be a fine opportunity for Boyce Puryear to talk her into seeing things his way, perhaps to take on the role of finally being her rescuer. But Puryear understood. He nodded slowly, but at first made no answer, his eyes narrowing as he considered the startling proposition.

"Your idea is plumb good, Putt," he said at last. "We've got to figure out how best to carry it out, of course, so there won't be any slip-ups, and—" He bent forward and spoke barely above a croaking whisper—"I have another idea to match it. Might as well do things up good and brown while we're at it. This one of mine concerns the Twin Springs section, and it's like this—"

For an hour the two talked in low voices, while an armed gunman sat just outside the shattered door. Two others occupied an adjoining room with the door open. Even as Puryear and his henchman talked they could hear the unusual activity that was going on in the streets outside, and the boss of Comal was satisfied with the sounds. His first action, on being released, had been to raise the ante on the money placed on one Ace Renfrow's head, not—as he had promised the day before—to two thousand dollars, but in a leap to five thousand.

That news had been speedily broadcast throughout the town and relayed to the surrounding ranches. As it spread, more and more groups of scalp hunters were riding out upon the search. The clatter of their horses' hoofs was sweet music to Boyce Puryear's ears. He congratulated himself on having made the right move. Men in and about Hondo recognized that five thousand dollars was fifty hundred *pesos—mucho dinero.*

Even knowing that a pack of snarling human wolves was on his trail did not keep the Cholla Kid in close hiding. But he kept well to the trees of the hillsides and the underbrush, riding no trails as he went on about a quiet, systematic, deadly search of his own. Given anything like a fair break, he meant to decimate the numbers of those hunting him when he saw them, with special attention to any man or men riding horses bearing the K Breeching K brand. He was not looking for open fight, but meant to make some discoveries, if possible, about Lynn Merrill's murder which had—according to Sanna-—already been made by some of her father's rancher friends.

It was perhaps half an hour before dusk when

Cholla, riding southeast across the Twin Springs patch, ascended a wooded hogback and suddenly reined in his cayuse. Motionless he watched for a moment what was going on down below him, his lips thinning and his eyes narrowing. From where he stopped, he was screened from below.

Twelve or fifteen men were down there, stringing up a three-strand barbed-wire fence across the Twin Springs range front. Some were spading holes and planting posts taken from a mule-drawn wagon. Others were using tampers and strung wire, section by section. And still others, mounted and armed with rifles, besides the guns that bristled at their belts, kept a watchful eye out. At the small cabin near the springs, a chuck wagon stood, and a cook was busily engaged in preparing supper.

Cholla savvied immediately. Boyce Puryear had taken possession of the Twin Springs ahead of time, confident that Sanna Merrill would not be able to hold onto the place. And now it would take gun-smoke to oust him.

There was red, boiling rage in the Cholla Kid's soul as he turned his pony, tied the mount a short distance down the slope in *cañada*—a deep gash in the hillside hidden by brush—and jerking the Winchester from its saddle boot, retraced his steps to the crest. Pockets filled with extra cartridges and a cold quirly stub between his lips, and hunkered down in a leafy covert, he studied the situation, making his decision as to the best spots to place his shots. Then deliberately he pressed the gun stock to his shoulder, and his finger curled around the trigger. It was long sniping, as he realized, but he had a prime rifle.

Confusion reigned down below at the first swift messenger sent from the Cholla Kid's weapon. Others followed before a breath could be taken. Cholla placed his shots swiftly and accurately, completely demoralizing the range jumpers who at the suddenness and unexpectedness of the attack could not at first even figure out the direction from which the rain of rifle fire was coming. Besides, they were in the open; Cholla was sheltered on the ridge, but he realized there was broken country behind him that was easily accessible. For him, in case of necessity; for others, if they could make it, it would afford a fine opportunity for closing in on him.

Cholla's first shot hit a mark, when a man leaped into the air, then banged the ground, clawing at the sod. A second man, tamping posts, was hit with one of the fast spray of bullets, and rolled along the ground, cursing and howling. A shot raked one of the wagon mules, and both animals lunged away on a dead run, rocking the wagon behind them, spilling half-loosened posts. Cholla fired again and again. Through his own rifle smoke he could see that a horse was down, kicking, as his rider flung from him. A second horse was rearing and bucking madly from a bullet sting.

The howling men below had placed the direction of the raking rifle fire by now, though, and were coming on the leap, spreading out as they came. Putt Ratliff was shouting orders, his arms waving toward the crest of the hogback. Cholla knew the meaning of that, and he had no intention of being caught in a *cul de sac*. Tearing down to the *cañada*, and leaping to the saddle, he was off and away toward the broken country before any of the range jumpers could possibly circle him—taking advantage of that stretch of wild country himself, where all Puryear's hired killers and their partisans could look for him all night without success.

But Cholla did not hole up in the badlands, as his pursuers were expecting, when finally they went glumly back to take stock of the damage he had done in a few devastating minutes. He waited awhile when he knew he was safe from pursuit, then went on to finish the chore he had begun. He rode a wide, swinging circle, and again approached Twin Springs—from the northwest this time.

Staking his mount well out of hearing from the line shack, Cholla began a wary stalk of the group gathered about a fire near the building. He saw Putt Ratliff get up and go into the cabin, stopping in the doorway to snap some instructions, and to yawn, his heavy arms stretched high. The Cholla Kid grinned grimly. Right into his hand. There went the man—alone—whom he most intended to get.

So cautious was Cholla's approach that the guard, stationed a distance from the fire and the shack, was not conscious that anyone was around until Cholla sprang. As the Kid's feet hit the ground he slashed the guard with his gun, at the same time crooking an elbow around the husky's throat and backheeling him to the ground. There came a strangled protest—then Cholla's gun flashed down against the fellow's skull. This time the guard subsided, limp and still.

Inside the shack, Putt Ratliff's eyes were on the ragged cot, his thoughts on the sleep for which he yearned. He heard the creak of the door as it opened, spun around, hand darting to hip, lips opened to yell. But his hand never reached his hip, nor was his voice raised. His pig eyes that had widened at the unexpected sight of the Cholla Kid closed at the same moment his shout was choked off when Cholla leaped, gun upraised, to smash it with all his force over Putt Ratliff's uncovered head.

Without a sound, Puryear's brutal foreman slumped to the floor and lay still, his face taut-drawn in the dim light, gray as ashes. Swiftly the Cholla Kid bound him and tossed him on the cot before he turned to the door, glancing out of it through a crack.

All unconscious that anything was wrong, the four men about the fire were still talking. Cholla Sutton took one long breath as both hands clutched tightly around his gun butts. He sprang outside the door, and on his movement red flames from both guns spat swift and sure toward the group around the fire.

Yells and shrieks of rage and pain split the early dark. Then men were running, scrambling to get out of the way of the flaming tornado that was upon them. Two of them lay doubled up by the fire, as Cholla's raking fire never stopped. He heard the clatter of horses' hoofs as those who had escaped, yelling their warning to others farther along and who turned and joined the escapers in a mad clatter, tore away from the death that had reared up suddenly beside their camp fire.

What was in their minds Cholla did not know— not until the story was later told of the wild tale brought to Boyce Puryear in Hondo the next morning. Silence was upon him as suddenly as the uproar had come. There was nothing left but the crackling of the flames and the patter of swiftly-withdrawing horses.

There was no time to waste, though, and much work to be done—or undone, rather. The clatter of the receding horses had not quite died away when Cholla leaped into action, busy with the scattered tools that had been left behind. Dark had completely fallen when he had completed his work of wreckage, and stood up, wiping the sweat from his brow. He glanced toward the cabin, wondering if his prisoner had regained consciousness, but did not go to look. Putt Ratliff was well tied up; he would not be able to work free.

Slowly the Kid turned his eyes, searching about the place. Not far from the cabin stood a lone cottonwood tree. Its limbs stretched gauntly toward the gray-black of the night sky. There were plenty of other such trees as that in that country, Cholla reflected, and after all this was Sanna Merrill's land and property. No need to contaminate it.

A cold, hard light was in the Cholla Kid's eyes as they turned from the tree and he made his way back to where he had left his horse. And as he started on his swift journey back to Jeff Kuykendall's ranch, his eyes held an icy thoughtfulness while through the fingers of one hand were slipping the cold, inexorable feel of his lariat.

Dawn came on, still gray and blustering. Boyce Puryear, ensconced in a new room at the Medina House in Hondo, and under heavy guard of his gunmen, rose early. He was expecting much to

228

happen this day. During it, there might be some memorable events. He was anxious, too, to hear a report from his men at Twin Springs as a starter.

Some of his news came more swiftly than he had expected—and was far from what he had so confidently planned. Breakfasting at the Chinese cafe across the plaza, he was interrupted by the arrival of a slickered, mud-spattered horseman who rode into town hell-for-leather.

Jumping from his kak before the hotel, the rider shot into it, and was immediately out again, plunging into the restaurant and up to Puryear's table.

"Boss, Putt Ratliff was murdered last night!" he burst out. "Don't know how come he was so far away from Twin Springs, but he was snaked up to the big cottonwood at Skull Crossin' on the river. His carcass was plumb loaded with lead, an' this here paper was pinned to his shirt."

He held out a square of brown paper, torn at one place with a round hole and stained a reddish brown. Printed with an indelible pencil, and still plainly legible, was the following gruesome message:

A WARNING FOR ALL MURDERERS
IN COMAL BASIN

Puryear crushed the stained placard in a big fist, his face working. There was little of

229

personal feeling in the man, but he had had an important engagement with Putt Ratliff for early this morning. Putt had been head man of all the plans, and it would necessitate the boss's taking others into fuller confidence now. Late yesterday afternoon the foreman had left Hondo for Twin Springs, to oversee matters there—riding alone. Now he was dead. Hanged—by whom? Was the act that black-headed lobo's or—?

But the messenger of ill omen had not half finished with his devastating news. He was talking again, rapidly.

"And that ain't all, boss," he said, his words tumbling over each other. "All hell broke loose over on the Twin Springs last night. The boys there was attacked by a big gang o' masked riders, an' none o' them remember anything about Putt after the big ruckus started. That gang, five or six to one o' them, took 'em plumb by surprise, was on 'em a-shootin' before they could lift a hand. Some of our boys got away an' made it back to the *rancho*, banged up a-plenty. Some never got back a-tall. Lanfear got rubbed out, along with plenty others . . . They made two attacks, them masked killers did, one just before dark when they was just a few of 'em first, snipin' from the hills. The boys run 'em off, an' wasn't expectin' 'em to come back. But they did—strong! The wagons were burned, the remuda scattered, and hell busted loose more'n plenty. All the fence strung yesterday was torn down, and some o' the best hosses killed. . . ." The messenger was panting as he spat it all out breathlessly. His voice rose to a wail as he finished. "It's time to do somethin', Boss, I tell you! We've *got* to do somethin'!"

"Go away!" choked Puryear, loosening his shirt collar, his face apoplectic. "Hit the trail! And send twelve men in here from the ranch as fast as they can fan the grit. *Do* something, you say? All right, cowboy! We'll do something all right. Today's the show-down!"

That was the first of the day's startling events which were to be far more memorable than Puryear had conceived when first he had planned for them.

CHAPTER XVIII
PURYEAR PLAYS TRUMPS

IT WAS about ten o'clock when there arrived in Hondo, a grim, determined-faced body of riders numbering seven. As they passed along the plaza toward the Stockmen's Bank, their progress was followed from windows and doors of the town by the eyes of curious, whispering watchers. Something was about to happen to Boyce Puryear's plans, was the general opinion. There was a tenseness, hushed voices, discussing what it might be, and what action the czar of Comal would take.

Every man in the party was well known. They were men with reputations as honest ranchers who long had defied the mandates of Puryear; who had resisted his ruthless tactics. The riders were Jeff Kuykendall, Kip Helm, Joe Kennedy, the Bar Lazy 3 Slash foreman, and Badger Harvey, Curly Bell and Jim Stone, Bar 3 punchers. All were stern and forbidding of countenance. With them rode Sanna Merrill.

Head erect, her cheeks touched with the color fanned into them by the morning breeze, wisps of her gold-brown hair blown from beneath her wide hat, her eyes were set ahead, but there was no sparkle in their blue. They were purposeful eyes. She looked neither to one side nor the other as she came ahead on her beautiful thoroughbred mare which had been one of her father's last gifts. At Sanna's own slender waist hung an ivory-mounted pistol. That the party this morning invading Hondo were determined of purpose was plain.

Boyce Puryear watched the cavalcade from a window of the Legal Tender. He made no comment when he saw it halt before the bank, and the girl, Kuykendall and Kip Helm pass inside. The other four punchers remained on their horses, gathered protectively about the bank front.

"She's got the money all right," Puryear said to himself. "It must have gone pretty straight from the Medina House to her."

His eyes swept toward the west side of the plaza expectantly. He turned from the window and went back to the bar, glanced at the impassive Creed Calkins.

"A drink," said Puryear. "And have one yourself." He had a clear mental vision of what was going on inside the Stockmen's Bank.

Luke Brundett, his vulpine face thinner and more parchment-like than ever, received the trio from Blanco country in silence. Indicating for them to sit down when they entered his private office, he pursed his lips and waited, fingers

234

pyramided. The president of the bank was not ignorant of all that had been going on.

Sanna Merrill did the talking. She began abruptly.

"I am not coming to you as empty-handed as before, Mr. Brundett," she said shortly. "I am here, ready to pay off the lien and mortgage on Twin Springs, due this morning. You know the exact amount, of course?"

Brundett shook his head a little uncertainly, and began to fumble with some papers. Sanna's crisp voice broke in:

"It isn't necessary to search," she announced. "I know what it is—twenty-seven hundred, fifty-six dollars, and thirty-two cents exactly. And here it is in cash."

Placing the exact amount on Brundett's desk, she asked for a receipt.

"The canceled mortgage and the lien, too, if you please," she said firmly, as her eyes for a quick moment met those of Jeff Kuykendall.

The bank official, face twisted, drew paper and pen toward him and started to write. Finished, he handed Sanna the receipt with a curt bow.

"You will have to wait until I see Mr. Puryear for the mortgage and lien," he said, his eyes shifting from the steady looks trained on him. "He has those in his lock box, since, as I told you before, he has taken them over. Probably he will be in town some time today, and I will get them for you then. This afternoon late, or some time tomorrow you can come by the bank and I will have them here for you, Miss Merrill. The receipt for this money deposited is ample protection for you—"

"Perhaps," said the girl coolly. "But I wish a deposit slip, Mr. Brundett. From the cashier, please."

Lines deepened on Brundett's face, from nose to mouth corners, and his lips grew thinner, if possible. But he got up and went to the door, spoke to the cashier and waited a moment, then came back and gave her the deposit slip without comment. Pocketing it, the girl arose.

"I'll get the canceled mortgage and lien in the morning," she said icily. Without even a good day, she left the place, with Kuykendall and Helm stalking along behind her.

The entire transaction had taken but a short time, and it was only some minutes past eleven when Sanna Merrill, Jeff Kuykendall and their five companions rode slowly out of Hondo, again without looking to right or to left. Zach Dagget, seated in a tipped-back chair outside the Legal Tender swinging doors, watched them depart, a sneer twisting his swollen and battered mouth. Too badly injured to take a hand in devilment and out of the running as far as active fighting was concerned, he was still able to do scout duty, and was on hand in case of an emergency when the boss of Comal should need every available man. His gross face darkening with hate, he spat tobacco juice after the departing cavalcade, the fingers of his left hand twitching.

"Two, three hours from now," he muttered, "you won't be so cocky, lady-bird! Wish I could be in on the fun, damn it!"

Three miles out of Hondo, the Encinal road took a sharp right-angle turn around a wooded ridge. The barranca bed was a talus of boulders and rock fragments, thickly matted with cactus and chaparral. The crowding slopes were dark with brush, and made darker by the cloudy, wct day. The overhanging sky was threatening a fresh downpour any minute.

Flanked by her armed guards, Sanna Merrill rode into that coulee all unsuspecting. And what happened in it, took place with the suddenness of a thunderbolt. With as reverberating reper-cussions as though the heavens themselves had opened.

Without a whisper of warning the air was dis-cordantly split by the slam and crash of rifles and six-guns. Bullets whizzed in a hail of death and destruction and flames cut through the lowering half-twilight. Sanna Merrill and her six com-panions, strung out in the coulee bottom, were caught in a trap. Each member of the bush-whackers, from his vantage point in the shielding chapparral, had selected his target, and did not miss. At the first volley, all six men were hit.

The unexpected savagery of the ambush dazed Sanna Merrill. At the first onslaught her throat was paralyzed beyond screaming.

By what at first seemed a miracle, she was unscathed in the hail of lead, but she saw men fall from their plunging mounts before her and a quick turn of her head saw others tumble from their horses in her rear. Vaguely then, with eyes filmed with horror, she saw many men bursting from the concealing bush on each side of the trail. Saw four riders making toward her from both ends of the cut.

Then the paralysis was out of her arm, her ivory-mounted gun was out of its holster and she was firing blindly at men who were coming on her in swarms. One of them leaped at her from behind, twisted the smoking weapon from her hand and flung it into the rocks. Unarmed, she was helpless. Utterly unnerved by what she had witnessed, she swayed in her saddle, clinging to the pommel with both hands.

A rope hissed through the air, looped over her head and jerked taut about her arms. A brutal-faced ruffian grabbed her mare's bridle-bit, jerking the nervous, highly-strung thorough-bred to a dancing standstill. The man who had disarmed her quickly tied her wrists behind her back. Still another, beetle-browed and bewhiskered, lashed her feet together with raw-hide thongs passed beneath her mount's belly. The men worked silently and swiftly, completely ignoring the moans of the injured men on the rocks or the still figures of others.

Forgetting herself as she saw her fallen companions, Sanna moaned, too, and tears sprang to her eyes as she saw the crumpled figure of Jeff Kuykendall, only a few feet ahead. Never again would that tall, stalwart ranchman come to her aid. The bushwhackers had done for him for good, and he lay sprawled grotesquely in the rocks, beside the body of his sorrel gelding from which he had been flung. Sanna caught a sight of the filming eyes of him who had been her father's, and her own, best friend. Kuykendall had been violently sent on the long trail, where he would meet and travel along once more with the wife he had so sorely missed.

There was no time for her to take stock of all the damage that had been done, what men had been killed, who still were living, for in less than three minutes her captors had her securely tied. Then they were in their saddles again. After hurrying their hidden horses from the brush, they were riding swiftly across the flats toward the Comal.

"You—you murderers!" flamed Sanna, finding her tongue at last as the tightening in her throat lessened with the increasing of her rage. "Those men back there—you killed them!—without giving them a chance!"

"They're not worryin' about you—*now,*" guffawed one of her bewhiskered captors, who rode stirrup to stirrup with her. "You needn't worry none about them!" He gave her a sharp glance. "And now that we can talk confidential like, without so much gunfire to interrupt our conversation, I'll just trouble you for that paper you got awhile ago at the bank, miss."

He reached out a hand and pulled rein on Sanna's mare as he drew in his own mount. Helpless, tears of rage dimming her eyes, Sanna watched the man fumble in her pocket and take the receipt and deposit slip which Brundett had given her. There was a sneering laugh of triumph on his thick lips as he shoved the pieces of paper into his own pocket. He hit her mare across the rump and they were off again.

Though such things as money and mortgages amounted to little right then in the face of the tragedy she had just witnessed, Sanna realized that with her receipt and deposit slip gone and the lien and mortgage still in the possession of Boyce Puryear, she was in as bad a fix as far as keeping her promise to her father to hold onto Twin Springs was concerned as she had been before she had paid the debt.

The bearded gun man at her side seemed to read her uneasy thoughts, for he showed his blackened teeth in a grin and chuckled meaningly.

"You can't play with the devil an' be afraid o' brimstone, lady," he said, but Sanna was not listening. Her thoughts were despairing ones. Where were they taking her now? And what did they intend to do with her?

CHAPTER XIX
CHOLLA DEALS A COLD HAND

DAWN of the morning when Sanna Merrill was so brutally abducted found the Cholla Kid in the foothills adjacent to the Rafter M. At his last conference with the friendly ranchmen, it had been considered best that he not risk sleeping under any hacienda roofs for the time being, because of the imminence of spies, so he had caught what sleep was necessary in the open. Wrapped in his poncho he had closed his eyes for a time in a small cave he found which was big enough to hide him and his pony.

But with the dawn he was awake, anxious to be on the prod again. The last thing that was in his mind as he ate his cold snack for breakfast, not daring to risk a fire, was that Sanna Merrill should now have any difficulty in holding onto her property. She had the money to pay her debts in full that morning. Why should she lose it?

He was not long to remain in ignorance of all that happened that gruesomely eventful morning. Shortly after sunup he was on his way again, keeping to the wooded places, riding by a devious route toward Jeff Kuykendall's spread. He was supposed to meet the rancher about noon, when the final plans were to be made to draw closed the net about the dry gulchers. It was already tightening.

He kept well in the greasewood and mesquite bosques that marked the line between the Rafter M and the far-reaching Lazy 3 Slash brands. Red Blake, the Slash *segundo*, had met up with him at a secluded rendezvous the afternoon before, and had told him of the five thousand dollars reward which Boyce Puryear was now offering for his scalp, and Cholla knew that only too many Basin denizens had marked him down for branding and were on a continued search for sign of him. Puryear had known what he was doing when he had dangled fifty thousand *pesos* before the greedy eyes of the rough element of that territory. So not for a moment did the Cholla Kid relax his vigilance.

It was a little after twelve o'clock when, sheltered in a scrub-covered cove, waiting for the time and proper opportunity to ride on to the Slash for his appointment, he saw a rider spurring hell-bent toward the Slash *hacienda*. The man was riding in from the Hondo road, and even at his distance, the Cholla Kid could see the foam that flecked the horseman's mount that had not been spared in miles. Cholla, who could smell trouble farther than a crow could fly, felt his nerves tighten.

Instinctively he knew, by that nagging of his sixth sense, that something had happened—something sinister and unexpected. Also he remembered how, early that morning, he had watched from where he had cached himself and his horse not far from the Rafter M hacienda and seen Jeff Kuykendall and some other punchers ride off with Sanna Merrill. Cholla had known they were accompanying her to town and what was her mission in Hondo. He added two and two, and distinctly did not like the answer.

No time to hide out now, waiting for the appointed time to meet Kuykendall. Something told the Cholla Kid that he was wanted down there below, at the Slash hacienda, and wanted at once. Without hesitation he touched spurs to the clay-bank and galloped straight for the ranch house, rifle loose in its scabbard, six-guns ready in their unfastened holsters.

It was there, from a breathless and incoherent Clover Leaf rider, that he learned of the ambuscade in the coulee, of Kuykendall's death and Sanna Merrill's abduction. The Cholla Kid came to a reared stop, with gravel flying, in time to hear the last words:

"And Gawd help us all," the man was pantingly shouting, "they got Jeff Kuykendall right through the heart—got your boss! *And the sidewinders carried off Sanna Merrill!*"

In the midst of shouted questions, muttered

threats against the perpetrators of the catastrophe, Lafe Starkey, the horseman who brought the message, managed to tell his story. He had, he said, been *en route* from town to his spread, after having spent the night in Hondo. He had caught up with a Cross H wagon and two cow punchers when he was not far out of town. They were bound for an outfit up the valley and he had ridden along with them. In a short time they had come upon the shambles in the arroyo—two dead men, and four badly wounded.

One of the dead men was Jeff Kuykendall, the other was Joe Kennedy, the Slash 3 foreman. The Cross H men were lugging the wounded men, including Kip Helm who did not want to be taken to the Rafter M, to the Slash ranch. They would arrive in a short time, as soon as the wagon could get them there. One rider was on his way back to Hondo after the doctor, and the Slash riders would have to go back to the arroyo for their dead boss and his foreman.

Lafe Starkey told all this in sections, but not until after he had told what to Cholla was most important of all—of the certainty of the men who had found the shambles that Sanna Merrill had been carried off.

"They got her, sure as guns," Starkey said glumly. "An' no tellin' what they mean to do next. We had to pay right quick attention to them wounded men, but one o' the boys rode along to the head o' the coulee and on a ways, lookin' for sign. There was plenty of it even without her gun we found in the rocks. From where the shootin' come off he could pick up the track o' Miss Sanna's mare, an' he picked 'em out of a lot o' tracks beyond—there was a whole raft o' murderin' skunks in that bushwhackin'—Lost all their tracks a little farther along, though, when the whole kit an' kaboodle took to the creek—"

Cholla Sutton listened with set and stony face. Red Blake, his freckled face working, cursed long and sulphurously. The few punchers who had heard Lafe Starkey's story had started off hell-bent, some of them for the bunk house, and the corrals, spreading the news, while others leaped on horses to carry it to the scattered riders who could be quickly rounded up.

But the Cholla Kid, stern and silent, made no comment—at first. He waited only long enough to speak a private word with the Slash *segundo* when Red Blake could be caught for a moment in his dashing about, shouting orders.

"I'm takin' the trail, Red," Cholla said tersely. "I'll find out someway, where they've taken Miss Sanna. We've got to get her—"

"An' we will!" blurted the fiery-haired *segundo*, as his gray eyes blazed. "If we have to smoke out every sidewinder in the Comal Basin."

"Right," said Cholla, and his lips tightened, though his voice was not raised in fury as was

247

Blake's. The anger of the Cholla Kid was too glacier-like, too deadly, for that. He said to the *segundo*:

"You savvy the bent cottonwood tree at Vereda ford on the Comal? The tree to the left o' the crossin'?"

Red Blake smiled grimly, with no trace of humor.

"Ought to," he snapped. "It's plumb close in my memory. I wasn't there last night when— when something, right justified happened, but I've been hearin', and if there was just a few more could be—"

Cholla stopped him with a curt nod.

"All right. Well, when I learn where they've taken Miss Sanna, I'll leave a message for you in the hollow above the first crotch. You can have all the boys you know're safe all ready to ride. *Sabe*?"

"I got you," said Red grimly. "The gang'll be gathered and ridin' anyway by two o'clock this afternoon, Cholla. We'll be ridin' right on your tail, shore. An' I'm thinkin' maybe they'll be more'n we count on . . . Somethin' funny— lissen—there must be some more hombres than we know into this thing—the boss didn't tell us much, but the story is there was a masked gang come down on them Twin Springs range jumpers just 'fore you come on Putt Ratliff tied up in that shack—"

The Cholla Kid did not give him any information. He only nodded bleakly as he said:

"I'll be lookin' out for you an' the other riders. See you later, Red. *Adios*."

Wheeling his horse, he headed out across the mesquite and sage flats for the southern horizon. An idea had suddenly come to him that one versed in the science could have told him had to do with criminal psychology. Knowing nothing of that, he merely followed an insistent instinct which told him that sooner or later some of the men who had worked murderously beside Putt Ratliff would unerringly drift to the spot where he had paid for his brutal crimes.

When he reached the Comal he veered eastward, following its course toward Skull Crossing, taking more precaution to keep hidden in the brush than ever. More than his personal safety was at stake now. Where the K Breeching K road forded the stream he crossed it. He saw the tree from which Putt Ratliff had swung, and after glancing at the wealth of sign underneath and round about—sign which K Breeching K riders would not long leave uninvestigated—he laired up and watched the road. He figured it would be only a short time before someone useful to his ends would pass by, would without question stop beneath that tree.

Neither psychology nor the Cholla Kid was wrong. Soon he spotted a lone horseman

249

cantering from the Hondo direction. He came toward the spot at a casual gait. The hip brand of the pony was K Breeching K. The Cholla Kid hunkered hard by the trail, gun ready, until the rider forded the still swollen stream and floundered up the north bank, coming straight toward the grim tree which stood as gray as funeral robes; and menacing.

His horse shied suddenly, and Poke Swanzy—for it was he, the man who had first recognized the Cholla Kid—found himself staring into the muzzle of a six-shooter. And into a face he knew at once, but which was hardly recognizable in its unbounded rage and thirst for vengeance.

Terrible was the word that alone could describe the face of the Cholla Kid since first he had heard of Sanna Merrill's abduction. And that word was woefully insufficient. The snarling rage that tore at his heart dwarfed the hate he had earlier felt for the men who had killed the girl's father and tried to pin the murder on the Cholla Kid. Those things were small compared with what now had been done. With Sanna Merrill in the hands of Boyce Puryear's brutes, Cholla's soul was steeped in killing madness. It showed in every line of his face.

"Gawdelmity!" Poke blurted, jerking his arms skyward at Cholla's bitten order. "You again?"

"In person," said Cholla, his lips twisting. "Mighty glad to meet up with you, hairpin. Just stay right still a minute till I pull your fangs." He jerked Poke's gun from its holster and prodded him in the back with his own six-shooter. "Now head on west a little ways along this river bank, and keep your gab buttoned up. I ain't got time to fool with you today."

The ruthless purpose and swift attack of the man he knew to be wanted by the authorities for dare-deviltry struck Poke like a sluice of ice water. Swallowing his Adam's apple and wetting cotton-dry lips, he led off as directed.

He had been bound from Hondo, carrying a message from Puryear to Bull Wickline, temporary foreman of the K Breeching K, in place of the lynched Putt Ratliff.

Poke knew all about that dry-gulching and kidnapping of this morning, too, for he had already met up with two of the renegades who had been in it. They had been cutting back to the ranch. Poke had followed the main trail, though, while the others had cut through the scrub.

What was uppermost in Poke's terrified mind now, was how much the Cholla Kid knew about the affair, and if he thought that Poke Swanzy had been among those present at the massacre in the coulee.

A short distance away from Vereda ford, Cholla called a halt and curtly ordered Poke to dismount.

"You white-livered coyote," he growled, "I'm not thinkin' you had nerve enough to be taken in with rattlers that's out for real killin's, so you can wipe some o' that chalk out o' your map. But you shore *are* a key that's goin' to unlock a lot o' things for me damn pronto," he added, his lips grim with meaning. He lifted his six-gun and held it trained on Poke Swanzy's middle. "Now you swill-eatin' polecat, spill everythin' you know about that wholesale killin' and kidnappin'—I'm sayin' here and now you know it all!—and don't try to cry ignorant on me!"

Fear gripped Poke's mind, made way for its brother, panic. He was helpless, fully cognizant of it, wholly at the mercy of this Cholla Kid, whose eyes spoke plainly of him knowing no mercy. Only once or twice he made an effort to cry out that he knew nothing, to attempt to save the men with whom he had holed-in. But the Cholla's levelled gun and his equally levelled eyes spoke more plainly than words. Babbling incoherently at last, Poke Swanzy told everything he knew.

Cholla was thoughtful for a moment after the young puncher had finished, his words trailing off into a plea for mercy.

"The Dry Arroyo Trail, and the hidden cabin, huh?" he mused.

He sensed, instinctively, that his captive was not lying. The Cholla Kid had had much reason to know men, to size them up. He could recognize a lie from verity.

"Mmm, a hideout in the Ramireñas. Yeah. About as I expected." He lifted his eyes to his captive's hang-dog face. "Now listen mighty careful, feller. Tell me just how to get there, and the best way to come up on the place easy like." His brows grew black, and his eyes steely. "And if I catch you lyin', you're goin' to wish you'd been born dead."

Protesting his veracity, Poke gave explicit directions. Then, barking a rough order, Cholla made him pass both his arms around the cottonwood bole, after which he tied Poke's wrists in half hitches. Shoving his legs in front of him and around the trunk of the tree of death, the Cholla Kid whipped the ankles of the frightened puncher together with a length of riata, locking Poke fast against the cottonwood. Pushing his captive further down on his left shank where there would be little danger of his being seen by a chance passerby, Cholla stepped back. He curled a brown paper cigarette and fanned it with deep relish.

Poke Swanzy was married to that cottonwood. Without another man's help he would never work himself free. With a hard chuckle, Cholla took paper and pencil from his pocket and wrote a rather long message to Red Blake. He placed it in the limb hollow far above Poke's head.

Without another glance at his prisoner, the Cholla Kid took time to hide the man's horse far back in a covert, ground-hitching him. That

253

range-trained pony would stand there until someone came for him. Then he got astride his own
horse and rode away. His eyes, fixed straight
ahead, were deadly steel, and in his heart was the
unquenchable anger that calls for somebody's
death.

CHAPTER XX
THE MOUNTAIN HIDEOUT

SANNA MERRILL did not know how far she and her captors had ridden, nor just where they might be headed, except that it was for somewhere in the Ramireñas. Hours passed and they still rode on. She imagined it was not such a distance as it seemed, for they were apparently taking a round-about direction, circling, sometimes doubling on their tracks, as she judged, taking to water when the opportunity offered, forcing their way through rough brush that tore at her clothing and caught at her hair.

She had thought she knew the whole country well, but they were taking her through a portion of it that was strange to her, rough, and weari-some. Long before they started to climb the steep hill trails she was exhausted, swaying in her saddle. The men with her made rough jokes, but none of them made an attempt to touch her nor to get close to her. That very fact had for her its ominousness. These men were working for Boyce Puryear, of course. He had given them their orders. And what did *he* want with her? What did he think he could gain by kidnapping her?

It was getting well along toward night, the shadows were deeper along the hillsides beneath the lowering clouds when the men riding ahead of her pushed their way through some heavier brush. Then she and the man beside her were following. They came out into a clearing. She recognized that place at once—not so very far from her own ranch. They had reached the "deserted cabin" which stood in one of the loneliest spots in the hills. Once she had visited the place with her father.

Weeds and scrub were growing high about doors and windows. There was a dim light in the cabin when the riders halted before it, and the bearded man riding beside Sanna got off his horse and unfastened her feet from beneath her horse. She shuddered when he lifted her off, trying to jerk away to help herself, but her legs were weak and stiff and she would have tumbled if he had not caught her.

"Easy, sister," he laughed. "But you'd ought to see they ain't much chance o' runnin' away on them legs, even if—"

He did not need to finish. Sanna knew how closely she would be guarded until whatever it was they intended to do should have been accomplished. It really could not be so much they could do to her, she tried to argue. Probably attempts would be made to force her to sign over the rights to the Rafter M itself to the grabbing boss of the Comal, but they would have their trouble for their pains. She set her teeth, determining to die as Jeff Kuykendall, as her father, had died before such a thing should happen.

The bearded man who had constituted himself her personal guard shoved her inside the shack ahead of him. The others got from their horses and drifted into the shadows already hovering about the cabin.

It was not lighted inside the shack, except for the one flickering candle on the crumbling mantelpiece. At first Sanna could see no one in the place at all, as her captor pushed her down on a rickety chair, her hands still tied behind her. She was glad of its support as her knees were still too weak to bear her weight. The bearded man said, with a sneering laugh:

"Pardon me if I leave you now, ma'am—there's somebody over there who'd like a word with you."

Sanna stared wildly about the dim room, like some hunted thing of those Ramireña fastnesses when the man went out, slamming the door behind him. Then somebody was getting up from a chair and coming toward her. She felt her blood chill to ice as she saw it was Boyce Puryear.

He came up to her chair and stood beside her.

"I'm afraid, Sanna," he said, his voice purring, "that some of my men, in their desire to avenge a comrade, have gone beyond their authority. I did not mean—"

"Don't try to tell me you didn't mean for them to kill Jeff Kuykendall, and bring me here to you a prisoner!" she flamed, struggling to get to her feet which failed her. "It's too obvious!"

"That's exactly what I do mean to say, my dear girl," Puryear went blandly on. "But it's a little late now to undo what's done. There is only one thing I can do—that is, to see that you are released, and—"

"Then why don't you do it—*now!*" she blazed, her anger beyond control. "If I could get away—run—if I could only *stand,* I'd—"

"Easy," said Puryear, in a soothing voice. "There are other considerations now, Sanna, things beyond either your control—or mine. You have been a witness to—ah—certain events . . . My men—I must stand by them, as they have stood by me. If you were to be released right now, it would mean that many of them would be hanged. I cannot allow that—I have my loyalty as you have yours. But—" He bent over to look into her angered eyes meaningly—"if you were to make certain promises, to see things in the right way, why—"

"There's nothing you can suggest to me, Boyce Puryear," Sanna tried to scream, but the very effort made her choke, "that would keep me from killing those men myself, the minute I can get a gun—and *you,* you murderer! *You* were the man who ordered the death of Jeff Kuykendall—just as I know you were responsible for my father's death! *What were you doing with his money belt?*"

Puryear's eyes narrowed, but he forced himself to keep up his even tone with her.

"You have been led to believe too many things—by a man known to have been a killer before he reached this Basin," he said. Before she could say anything in defense of the Cholla Kid, as he knew she would, he hurried on: "There is only one way out of this thing, now, Sanna, since certain things have happened that I could not stop. I have suggested it to you before—marry me, and you will never again be in danger. The men who have done this thing today—rough men who thought only of avenging Putt Ratliff—well, I'll promise you I will attend to them. In my own way. Comal Basin will never hear of them again . . ."

Her eyes filled with black rage, Sanna tried to struggle to her feet, fell back in the chair panting, almost incoherent. But she managed to spit out at the man:

"Marry you? Marry *you?* I'd rather think of marrying Satan himself! I—I—"

"You're beautiful when you look like that, my dear," Puryear said with a leering smile. "I like the fight in those blue eyes of yours, though you ought to be smiling at me for wanting to make your battles mine."

Chuckling, he bent and kissed the girl sitting in the chair, with her arms tied behind her. Then he reached back of her and deftly cut the thongs which bound her wrists.

"Don't say that I never did anything for you," he grinned. "You'll be wanting something to eat and you'll find it over there on the table. But," he added, as he moved toward the door, while Sanna's hands fell limply at her sides, "I wouldn't advise any trying to get out—not until after I come back and we talk this thing over some more—*after* you've had a chance to think about it."

He opened the door and slipped out, slamming it after him, even as Sanna's lips were trying to frame the worst word of which she could think to characterize him.

"Buzzard!" she cried, but Puryear's mocking laugh came back to her as she heard him giving some terse orders to some men outside. She was as tightly penned in that rickety cabin as though she had been in the strongest jail, and she knew it.

Slowly, as the blood crept back into her arms she lifted them and buried her head in them. The tears came freely at last. She was not conscious that her heart was calling out for help for any one particular man in the world, but it was. It was beating madly to the rhythm of "Cholla."

Travelling fast after he had left the tree where Putt Ratliff had swung, the Cholla Kid rode a wide, swinging circle, following side coulees and hugging the shoulders of hogbacks. There was never a moment when his trail-wise eyes failed to record the signs written on the earth, or the portents in the sky.

Winding up and down, he made his way nearer and nearer to the Ramireñas, led by instinct more than by any directions or maps over a trailless way that was in no way marked for the uninitiated. Down coulees, into basins, half-valleys, hidden in the badlands. Up again and through wild terrain, an outlaw country—a jumble of bare and broken hills leading to the higher wooded stretches far beyond—through dry washes, crumbling cutbanks, and coming unexpectedly through deep brush into hidden coulees. A country well fitted by Nature herself for men who wanted to get beyond the arm of the law, if law there had been in the Comal Basin, worthy of the name. The country through which the Cholla Kid rode he recognized at once as a hideout country beyond the law—a place where badmen might have foregathered even before they had a champion in Boyce Puryear who had need of their reckless guns.

He had been riding a long time, not certain of just where he was, trying to follow the blurted instructions of Poke Swanzy. Dusk had long since fallen, the sun going down with only an angry red fringe on the gray horizon clouds to show that it had appeared at all that day, or was reluctantly giving way to the lowering clouds and imminent drizzle. Night had come on, black as the ace of spades, and Cholla went on, leaving much to his sure-footed pony. He was wishing with all his heart for Jerky who surely would know instinctively where his master wanted to go.

It was almost ten o'clock when he halted sharply in the veiling black, quartering the breeze, like a hunting dog. A stray thread of smoke wove through that breeze—the odor of burnt wood—and Cholla was downwind.

Making no slightest sound, he got from his horse. Leaving the hard-ridden pony ground-hitched in a pinon-filled hollow, he crept forward toward a blurred outline that lifted against the sky across which now a crisp wind was sifting the clouds, leaving bits of it, star dusted, as a background for dim silhouettes.

As silently as any padded-foot night-prowling animal, or moccasined Indian who once may have roamed the same country, the Cholla Kid went inexorably on in his search. His nostrils quivered like those of a blood hound whose sensitive nose has just picked up the scent. But he was as deadly as a cougar hanging over his prey, ready to drop.

On the rim of a long, narrow bowl he halted, eyes straining to rake the inky pool of dark below. A smudgey patch of red and violet light pulsed in the canyon; the embers of a dying fire. And from what Cholla could see of the wall of rock beneath him, it fell sheer for some forty feet to a sloping, brush-covered bench.

Poke Swanzy had not lied, Cholla reflected grimly, even if his instructions had been more or less vague for a man unacquainted with the country. By keeping to parallel coulees and swales, as well as by allowing his instinctive sense of direction to have full sway, he had been able to track the Dry Arroyo Trail without running across any posted guards. Without question they were swarming on all the obvious sides of approach. Luck—and Fate—had allowed him to slip upon the hideout from what was possibly the one unguarded side, for the simple reason that it would be considered inaccessible.

A short search located a gnarled pin oak that grew on the canyon's rim. Uncoiling the long riata which he had wound about his waist, Cholla lashed one end about the oak and tossed the rope over the edge. With a chuckle, he gave low voice to the cowboy's time-honored expression of perseverance.

"Never get to the hills by lookin' at 'em," he muttered. "Here goes!"

Swinging himself over the rim, he snaked downward hand over hand, swinging perilously. The riata did not reach clear to the bench, he discovered, when his eyes, more accustomed to the star dimness, showed it to him feet below. It lacked what looked like some six feet, but swinging at the end of the leather hold, Cholla let go and dropped, frog-fashion, landing springily and leaping instantly to his feet. The jar dislodged a small avalanche of shale and rocks, but Cholla did not hesitate. The bench was still some distance up from the shadow that marked the cabin and the smear of what had been a camp fire, but he went on, clambering down, holding to what small growths met his clutch until he reached what felt like solid ground.

In the gloom, he could not expect to pick out men. He could discern only flickering, elusive shadows. Darting from what cover to cover offered—unexpectedly upstanding rocks, chaparral, bunches of grass behind which he could fling himself prone—he made his way toward the looming bulk of the shack.

Ever so often, as a matter of prudence, he dropped to hands and knees and remained motionless, listening, as his eyes strained to scan his surroundings. No sounds came to show he had been heard, and within a few feet of the cabin he lifted, bent almost double and boldly skimmed along toward it, guided by the dim light that flickered through a window.

Cholla made the rear of the cabin undetected. Surely Sanna would be inside, he prayed. He could see no other buildings. Behind it, against the bluff, was a pole corral. The sound of feeding horses came from it. Dropped now to hands and knees, the Cholla Kid approached the dark hut, hugging the ground between the cabin and the corral. Where in hell was all the gang, anyhow?

He learned the answer to that unspoken question in short order. From the bench from which he had so recently dropped came a shrill, high cry.

"Hey, boss! *Boss!* Somebody's come Injun on us! Somebody's down there! I just come up on his hoss a little ways back!"

"Yeah," gritted Cholla Sutton, as every nerve and muscle in his wiry, husky body tensed for action. "And the devil take the hindmost!"

He was in for it now—knew it! No need for further skulking. It was a time for swift exploits. The echo of the warning cry had not died away before Cholla Sutton was in motion, brain working even more swiftly than straining muscles.

He reached the front corner of the cabin wall just as the outlaw who had been squatting in front of the door, aroused by the shouts from above, lunged toward the same edge of the shack. They crashed heavily together, with the pung of muscle and bone crunching against the hardness of a like frame.

A spurt of flame licked out in Cholla's face, but the bullet of the attacking busky sang wild. Cholla's own gun, jammed against the fellow's side in the instant of the crash of their bodies, jerked with a roar. The man's loud curse rang out, smothered to nothingness as quickly, as he pitched against the wall and slid earthward, his cry choked by a mouthful of blood.

And even as he leapt away toward the door, Cholla heard Sanna Merrill's voice scream from inside the shack. He gained the door just as the man who had been reclining on his tarp roll on the crumbling doorstep sprang inside and was swinging the door shut.

Hurling his strong young body against it, the Cholla Kid carried both door and man inward, saving the door from being torn from its hinges by the fraction of an inch. He stumbled, then righted himself, as the outlaw gained his feet first and his gun blazed and thundered.

A searing fire passed across Cholla's right shoulder, but he paid it no attention. Sprawled on knees and left hand, he loosed three swift shots around the gun flash, all that he could see since the candle had given one last flicker and died from the swift draught of the door. There came

266

the sound of a sobbing breath, then the choky words:

"You—got me! Don't—don't—shoot—"

Cholla slammed shut the door behind him as he leaped to his feet, dropped the bar across it instantaneously, and heeled around. In a far corner he could hear the girl's convulsive breathing.

"Steady, Sanna!" he said hoarsely. "And don't get near that window."

"Cholla!" came her half-inarticulate cry. "Oh, Cholla! I *knew* you'd come! I knew it!"

"Yeah," said the Cholla Kid grimly. "And here's where we sit out the next deal!"

Someway, he could not have told how, he was across the room and beside her. His arms were groping out for her, as his voice choked:

"Sanna! Where are you? Where are you?"

A muffled gurgling cry greeted him as her hands touched him, and then she was in his arms.

"Oh, Cholla!" She raised her hurt arms stiffly and clung with them about his neck. Her head buried itself on his shoulder as wild tears came.

For an instant that might have been eternity, that could not be spared in their present predicament, he pressed her close and felt her heart beating wildly against his own. It might be for the first, last, and only time, but it was worth a lifetime of waiting, fighting for.

"Sanna," he choked, trying to speak naturally,

but failing miserably. "Have they—hurt you? I'll—"

Sounds from outside tore him away from her, brought him to a fighting crouch. A battle must be fought, and that instant of forgetting which had been all of life itself, had jerked him emotionally away from the realization of their all too perilous position.

There was no time for talk. No time for anything but the action that was imperative in fighting the peril bearing down on them from outside. They were in a jam, the devil of a jam—two of them penned here in the shack, with no hope of any outside aid coming to them soon. And heaven knew how many hombres, besides Boyce Puryear, outside craving to rout them!

Sanna's voice was sobbing, in spite of her effort to keep it calm.

"It was—it *is*—Puryear, Cholla!" she jerked out to him in the instant of realization of the peril at hand. "He's a devil!"

"All of that, Sanna," the Kid's voice came back to her. "All of it. But sometimes even hell itself can't beat two fightin' pardners!"

CHAPTER XXI
SNARLING GUNS

FROM outside the shack came yells, curses, the sound of running feet in clomping boots. Guns banged as the stout door, still miraculously on its hinges and reinforced by the heavy bar, thucked with a rain of bullets. The grimy glass in the single window shivered to a hundred fragments and tinkled on the floor as the drove of slugs whistled through and buried themselves against the opposite wall.

Cholla's breath came sibilantly in the repetition of his warning:

"Keep away from the line of that window, Sanna! Hug the wall!"

He had crouched instinctively when he had flung away from the girl, and he had started to get up from his half-kneeling position when from out of the dark two hands grasped his shoulders. For one wild, mad moment he felt Sanna Merrill's breath on his face. Her lips crushed against his in the voluntary surrender of a woman to the one man with whom she would live and die.

"I knew you'd come to me somehow," she whispered again. "You must have heard my call!" Her soft lips crushed back her own words. Then she straightened. "Give me that devil's gun you took away from him, Cholla!" she finished abruptly. "They'll never take me alive—again! Not—not with that Boyce Puryear out there waiting!"

No, the Cholla Kid savagely swore to himself, they would not—not if he could help it. If they did it would have to be over his dead body.

He wheeled again, crouched low in the dark, listening, trying to make out from the scurry of sounds outside when momentarily the gunfire stopped, just what they intended to do next. His fingers were taut on his guns, his eyes, in the dark, narrowed to slits. Out beyond that door was a pack ready to strike; to reach across his smashed body and lay hands on Sanna Merrill.

Well, it would have to be when his eyes were glazed, and his hands could no longer hold a gun. Not otherwise. And before that could happen, entrenched as he was, there would be fight— plenty. Even if they tore down the door with a battering ram.

Cholla held his fire. The shooting from outside began again with a deadly certainty. Men's yells and shouts were interspersed with the bullets that hammered at the door, snarled through the window, whining to their spent end in the log walls.

In the darkness, and without any sniping

through the ripped and smashed window to hold them back, his assailants had been able gradually to creep up close, snaking along on their bellies as he knew they would. The range of the bullets that smashed through the window showed him that.

Some of the men now were close enough that he could hear them as they pounded outside, working chinking between the logs, so that soon they would be able to rake the interior of the shack with cross fire. Boyce Puryear must have gone as hogwild as the rest of them, or he would not have allowed Sanna's life to be so jeopardized. Or perhaps he had given up all hope of her ever giving in to his demands, and, knowing that it was the Cholla Kid who was inside with her, he was seeking a double revenge. He would rather see her dead than in the arms of another. And it was to be remembered that with Sanna Merrill out of the way the boss of Comal could still achieve his ambition of owning the most prosperous part of the Basin which had not yet fallen into his hands.

Cholla was certain of his surmise that Puryear knew it was he who had come to Sanna's rescue when he heard the maddened bellow of the big boss from outside:

"Got you now, you hellion! Damn you, damn you! You've slipped through every trap I've laid for you! You think you've taken that girl from me! You'll find yourself in her arms in hell! Now see if you can slip out of this trap! I've got you cold turkey!"

For what seemed a lifetime, but which in reality could not have been more than minutes, the firing kept up. Then another sound came to Cholla's ears. One far more ominous, and which he had thought of first when he had sworn to protect Sanna with his life. Suddenly a heavy object banged against the door, shaking it jarringly. Puryear's bull bellow accented each thump of what was apparently a heavy log hastily hunted out for the purpose.

"Got you, got you! What're you goin' to do *now!*" It roared above the bedlam in maddened repetition.

For minutes more—another eon—the firing and the battering at the door continued furiously, then as suddenly it slackened, as the yells outside died to a confused murmur. Only random shots zipped through the window. That was confusing to the Cholla Kid and to Sanna, neither of whom had so far been touched even by a ricocheted shot.

Out of the darkness Sanna spoke.

"Ours isn't much of a gambling chance, is it?" she said quietly.

As quietly Cholla answered her:

"Not much. I won't lie to you, Sanna. It's a Chinaman's chance we've got. No more."

"I know." Someway, he did not know how,

the girl was beside Cholla, and he felt her hand touch his cheek. Then her warm arm was about his neck, her cheek was against his and she was whispering: "But—but if we do have to take the long trail, Cholla—well, we'll take it together. As it must have been intended, though somehow we didn't seem to find each other in time."

"It's not a bad trail to take—together—Sanna," Cholla whispered. "Up there a-ridin' along the Milky Way, and there'll be some we know a-waitin' to show us the way."

He heard the sob that caught in her throat and his hand clung to her tightly for a moment. Then she said, steadily:

"I—I just wanted to say—thanks for everything, Cholla. Thanks more than I can say—right now—for trying your best—and all the rest."

It was not a moment for many words. The Cholla Kid said what he had to say quickly, with a fullness of meaning it might have been impossible, under other circumstances, for him to have put across in all his life.

"Yeah. Okay. And—and just in case, Sanna—I reckon you know how I feel about you, even if I haven't said anything. I was waitin' for the chance—" He swallowed hard. Even in those tragic minutes it was difficult for the Cholla Kid, in all of whose devil-may-care life there had been no place for sentiment, to say the actual words that spoke his heart. But he did. "I love you,

Sanna," he said simply. Her softly caught sob answered him:

"I love you, Cholla. I've loved you from the first minute you spoke to me . . . Only it didn't take me so long to find it out."

His hand was gripping hers as there trembled between them the kiss that was meant for a goodbye until eternity. Suddenly the Cholla Kid tensed, sniffing the air like a hound. What he smelled electrified him back into fighting life. Smoke! The girl had smelled it, too, but she took it philosophically.

"They're burning us out, Cholla," she said calmly. "We won't have to wait long for the end. It will be only a short time until— Look! It's already starting through the back wall!"

She was right. As Cholla whirled to look, he saw a tongue of flame licking between the logs at the far end of the cabin. *That* accounted for the sudden ceasing of the fire outside, with only the sporadic sniping at the windows. Boyce Puryear had decided to play his game to its most tragic finish, regardless of the girl he had wanted to force to marry him. She had finally refused him— All right! His bitter vengeance was to be on her head and the man he knew she wanted.

Even as he saw the first lick of flame, the Cholla Kid knew that Sanna was right. It could not be long now. The seasoned cottonwood of which the shack was built would burn like tinder.

The sod roof would only intensify the billowing smoke and heat inside. There was no water anywhere near the shack for a long way down the ravine. Even if Red Blake and his men should come, there was nothing they could do—in time.

Cholla smiled crookedly, hefting his guns in each hand. The Blanco vigilantes would come, he was sure of that, but they would come too late, after all.

His hand reached out to grip Sanna's once more, and there was a hint of his old spirit in his voice as he said to her:

"Well, nothin' ever beat a try but a flop, after all, Sanna. It's up to us to make our big try."

As the flames grew and mounted and smoke billowed inside the hut, a rattling fusillade of bullets again drove against the door and through the window. The K Breeching K *paisanos*, urged on by this brutal master, doubly maddened to insanity through the failure of his plans, intended to cut the pair in the cabin down without a chance as they burst from the burning cabin, when they were no longer able to stand the smoke and the flames.

Cholla Sutton, his face like granite, threw back the bar before the door that held back the enemy.

"Last ditch, honey," he chokingly said over his shoulder to Sanna. "I'm smokin' a way out for you. Follow me, and keep your gun *ready!*"

Before Sanna Merrill could protest, before

275

her bewildered mind could quite grasp what the Cholla Kid was up to, he threw open the door. Smoke poured out in a swirling fog, obscuring the door opening for a moment, hiding the man. In the midst of the smoke went the Cholla Kid, weaving his way along the wall with his smoke covering. The bullets that sleeted through the door failed to slap him as he dove outside, and crouched and slithered against the outer wall, guns in each hand.

Throat burning and eyes smarting, half blinded, he made the end of the wall. A vague figure loomed ahead; there came a warning yell. Two guns, one of them the Cholla Kid's, crashed almost together, but it was not Cholla who went down. It was the smoke-clouded figure of the renegade who had made the onslaught who pitched earthward. Instantly there was an uproar of firing and yelling, spurts of flame cutting through the smoke that obscured vision, giving men no idea of where to place their bullets.

The whine and sing of them swarmed all about Cholla. In return his own guns spat scarlet at wavering phantoms who danced crazily in the whirling smoke. Groans and curses of pain sounded as his bullets scored and targeted. Then suddenly he burst out of the gloom of smoke, to find enemies all about him. A thrill stung him at the realization. He could not now misplace a shot and hit any friend. His guns could spit until there was no bullets left, and then— And the girl ought to be clear by now—

A new tone suddenly came to the yelling, taking on fright and terror. Before had been only triumph. It was breaking out in a roar beyond the fire embers, beyond the smoke that swirled in ever reddening eddies.

Spun completely around by a bullet that glanced off his cartridge belt, Cholla crouched close to the ground, wheeling on the balls of his feet, his pistols hammering death to their last bullet. His left shoulder was wet and sticky, and with a feeling of despair that he, too, was spent, he felt his arm growing numb. A bullet had singed his scalp just above an ear, bloodying him, making him feel sick and dizzy. A third cut his rawhide coat between ribs and armpit. His last cartridge was shot, but hastily thumbing in fresh ones as he crouched, weaving from side to side, he peered ahead, squinting uncertainly.

New hope surged in his heart at what he saw. Horsemen were charging into the light circle, shooting, yelling as they came, riding down the gunmen who were afoot. The horde of attackers of the cabin were being rudely scattered, their onslaughts shattered by the Blanco vigilantes who had arrived unheralded and unsuspected during the mêlée. The drum of their horses' hoofs had been drowned by K Breeching K gunfire, and the yells of a too-soon-acclaimed victory.

Killing the guards at the gap, the men who had been gathered together by Bart Lacey and Red Blake had come. They had swarmed on through and into the valley, riding like demons as the rising smoke and heavenward-shooting flames from the fired shack guided their course.

The moment before his newly loaded six-guns spoke again, the Cholla Kid heard above the uproar, the bellow of Bart Lacey, the angered war howl of Red Blake:

"Stretch those hosses' bellies! There's hell goin' on at the shack!"

CHAPTER XXII

HEADIN' HOME

IT WAS all over but the shouting, then, when the Blanco vigilantes swooped into the isolated clearing with yells and blazing guns. Boyce Puryear's men were fighters by profession, but they were also battle-wise. They knew when the odds were against them.

With this quick turn of events, it was very doubtful to them if further loyalty to the one-time boss of Comal would be rewarded. They had their own skins to save, too, and damn little time to do that. From the hill-encircled clearing there was no possibility of escape by horseback except by the one trail which Bart Lacey's and Red Blake's men now had well bottled up. The scrimmage had lasted but brief minutes, with slashes of gun-fire cutting the smoke-filled, reddened air, with war shouts above the crackling of the flames. Then the renegades turned tail and were scrambling toward the brush and the steep hillsides in the rear.

Those who stood their ground were quickly killed off. The handful of survivors, instantaneously sizing up the situation, first made for their horses to cut stick, only to abandon them on the run. It was a complete rout.

A few, a very few, managed to escape on foot. The others were granted scant mercy, for the Blanco men still held too vividly in their minds the bushing of Jeff Kuykendall and his riders, the killing and robbing of Lynn Merrill. There was no question here of who was guilty or not guilty. Every man in the clearing condemned himself by being there. It was not a pretty scene, there in Coyotero Valley that night.

Cholla Sutton stood in the glare of the burning cabin, guns hanging in weary hands, unconscious of his wounds as he watched the mop-up. The sudden let-down of spent energy left him gaunt and hollow-eyed, but triumphant. It was thus that Sanna Merrill found him when she ran from her hiding place in the bushes not far back from the wall of the burning hut.

He felt a soft cheek against his and two arms tighten convulsively around him.

"Cholla—Cholla Sutton!" came her tear-choked whisper. "It's all going to come true, after all! There *is* going to be a tonight and a tomorrow, Cholla!"

Smiling down into her tear-stained face, Cholla held her close. The feel of her strong young body sent maddening riot through his veins; the touch of that wet cheek against his whispered of days to come and of other nights. It was so that Bart Lacey found them when he rode up.

"Gawdelmity!" he said, wiping a sweat- and smoke-stained face. "However did you keep from bein' shot to doll rags, Cholla?"

"You can't kill an hombre that wasn't tagged to be killed," grinned Cholla.

"But he's hurt!" cried Sanna, for the first time appearing to see the blood that stained Cholla's face and stiffened his clothing. "We've got to get him away from here—quick!"

"We will," assured Lacey. "Pronto. There ain't much left here to be done. . . ."

Boyce Puryear, captured unwounded from where he was attempting to escape by climbing to the shelf behind the burning shack, was dragged into the fire glare. His naturally ruddy face was ghastly. He expected no quarter from these men to whom he and his men had shown none.

Zach Dagget, who had ridden from Hondo with him that afternoon, to be "in on the fun" to at least some extent, flanked the cringing ex-boss. Bowdre, the man who had tied Sanna Merrill and been her personal guard, was dead. Others, shot to ribbons by the infuriated vigilantes, lay all about in grotesque heaps, lit up by the fire. All told, there were but five prisoners. And the grim vigilantes from the Blanco country did not intend to waste any time upon their captives.

Ropes were jerked from saddles, as the highest

trees in Coyotero were inspected. The money receipt and deposit slip belonging to Sanna were taken from Puryear, who, crazed with terror, was pleading brokenly for his life—though he well knew that the easiest thing that could happen to him would be a quick rope which would swing him then and there into eternity, abruptly putting an end to the career of Comal County's cattle baron, political boss and range hog.

Zach Dagget was pleading, too. His brutal visage hideous, he also begged for his life.

"Don't hang me, fellers!" he gasped. "Don't! I'll tell you anything you want to know!"

"There ain't nothin' you can tell us that we don't already know," said Bart Lacey coldly. "Except, maybe, who killed and robbed Lynn Merrill."

"Shore I'll tell!" Dagget screeched, through the bruised lips that were a memento from the Cholla Kid. "It was Putt Ratliff, Wiz Stokes, Jake Bozeman, Yick Comer, Pasco Buck, an' Fingers McCall. I was scoutin' for 'em, but Gawd's truth, I wasn't there when it happened—I was on my way back to Hondo an' I didn't know they meant to kill him—only to get the money from him. But they killed him, too, before they brung the *dinero* back to Puryear. 'Twas Puryear, too, put Sheriff Swinton up to tryin' to shoot Renfrow. All of 'em that done the killin's are dead an' in hell now!"

"And they'll soon have more company," said Lacey grimly. "Grab holt, neighbors, an' let's start these jiggers a-dancin'."

Puryear's face was like ashes, wet and drab, but his teeth were clenched. Only Zach Dagget's voice rose shrilly, screaming for mercy. To where the Cholla Kid had led Sanna out of sight of the vigilantes, Zach's voice penetrated, howling her name.

"Miss Sanna! Miss Sanna! Don't let 'em! Don't!"

Before Cholla could detain her, she had pulled loose from him and was darting toward the men holding their ominous riatas. Her face was wild in the dancing firelight. She ran to Bart Lacey, clutching his arms, but her voice was chokingly quiet when she said:

"He's right, Bart! We must not do this terrible thing—not this way! Dad would not have wanted it, nor would Jeff. . . . Leave them to the law, Bart—we're going to have the right kind of law in Comal now!"

There were murmurs from the vigilantes, their blood lust unassuaged, but Sanna clung tightly to the man who led them, pleading that they not put themselves beyond the law in their thirst for vengeance. Bart Lacey looked down into her eyes a long minute, his lips tight, then he flung out an order.

"All right, neighbors! Reckon she's right at

283

that. Tie up them sidewinders—tight!—and let's be on our way."

Though there were mutterings, the order was quickly obeyed. In short time, Boyce Puryear and Zach Dagget were tied to their horses, flat on their backs, looking at the reddened sky. The last three buskies who had been taken alive came next, and what still was in store for them made them wish heartily they lay on the ground by the side of their luckier companions whose sightless eyes stared at the same dark sky.

It was a clean-up. Clean-up of all the Puryear gang except Poke Swanzy, who, released by the vigilantes at Vedero crossing and forced to accompany them to the canyon, escaped in the mêlée and had long since ridden hell-for-leather to Hondo.

He lingered there only long enough to get a fresh mount and to warn Creed Calkins of the debacle. Creed, roused from slumber, scratched his bearded jaw a moment, then shucked into his clothes, as Poke tore off to give his same warning to Luke Brundett.

"Creed," the saloon man said solemnly to himself, "the San Marcos trail leads plumb out o' Comal County. If you ride like hell an' don't stop to eat, you can make Marco by dark. *Adios*, Hondo."

Ten minutes later his horse was churning the dust eastward. . . .

Back in Coyotero Canyon, the vigilantes were getting ready to depart, taking their bound prisoners with them. Their work was finished. Comal County would once again be safe for honest folk. There would be a new county attorney, a new sheriff, a mayor of Hondo. A new bank president and a town marshal.

Sanna Merrill and Cholla Sutton, standing by their horses, looked at each other a long, long moment. The rest of the riders kept at a discreet distance. Then Sanna suddenly spoke, slowly.

"In the beginning, Cholla," she said, "I told you to take the ranch, to take me, to do what you wanted to with any or all of it. That still goes."

Cholla grinned at her from his smeared face, but his eyes were serious.

"I'm through saddle trampin', honey," he said abruptly. "Think I'll try raisin' cows instead o' hell for a change—when I've straightened up a few things in the Panhandle. I've got a dad back in Neuva Mex who'll be plumb glad to hear I've decided to chuck the stuff. He always said I was born to hang or born to succeed, but up to now it looked like the hemp had the best start."

"Cholla," said Sanna, "what you need is so much trouble on your hands you won't have time to get jittery."

"Dang near the truth," admitted Cholla, with a dry grin. "What would you suggest, Miss Sanna Merrill?"

"Ask me to marry you," she replied promptly. "I'd take you up, and make enough trouble to keep you busy for the next fifty years."

"You bought a maverick, honey," said Cholla, not hiding the joy in his voice. "I'm takin' *you* up!"

One arm went about her shoulders as Bart Lacey rode up, clearing his throat and coughing loudly.

"Hey," he blustered. "You two goin' to camp here all night? It's a long ride back to the bailiwicks—and the fellers with the prisoners must be halfway to Hondo by now."

"Comin' right away," said Cholla, as he lifted a foot to his stirrup. He took time for one swift thought that tomorrow it would be Jerky he would be bestriding. "And—thanks, *mucho*, Lacey. We owe you boys plenty for this night's work."

"Owe us nothin' a-tall," snorted Bart. "See you in town, maybe?"

"Tomorrow," nodded Cholla, as he swung on his horse. "Yeah."

"No—today," contradicted Sanna, as she leaned from her saddle to catch Cholla's hand.

"Huh?" asked Cholla, surprised. "Today?"

Sanna nodded.

"Yes, today," she said positively. In full view of Bart Lacey and his riders, she leaned farther over and kissed Cholla Sutton on the mouth.

"There isn't any minister out near the Rafter M," she said softly, "so it's Hondo, isn't it?"

"Yeah," the Cholla Kid said. "Sure enough, Sanna. I'll tell the world it's Hondo. We're headin' wherever there's a minister. . . ."

Center Point Large Print
600 Brooks Road / PO Box 1
Thorndike, ME 04986-0001 USA

(207) 568-3717

US & Canada:
1 800 929-9108
www.centerpointlargeprint.com